D1443062

PROJECT F

ALSO BY JEANNE DuPRAU

The Books of Ember

PROJECT F

Jeanne DuPrau

Random House 🏠 New York

This is a work of fiction. Names, characters, places, and incidents either are the product of the author's imagination or are used fictitiously. Any resemblance to actual persons, living or dead, events, or locales is entirely coincidental.

Text copyright © 2023 by Jeanne DuPrau
Jacket art copyright © 2023 by Leo Nickolls

All rights reserved. Published in the United States by Random House Children's Books, a division of Penguin Random House LLC, New York.

Random House and the colophon are registered trademarks of Penguin Random House LLC.

Visit us on the Web! rhcbooks.com

Educators and librarians, for a variety of teaching tools, visit us at
RHTeachersLibrarians.com

Library of Congress Cataloging-in-Publication Data
Name: DuPrau, Jeanne, author.
Title: Project F / Jeanne DuPrau.
Description: First edition. | New York: Random House Children's Books, [2023] |
Summary: Several hundred years in the future, in a world where fossil fuels
are no longer used as a power source, a thirteen-year-old boy named Keith
joins a jet pack project that will give people the ability to fly.
Identifiers: LCCN 2022033200 (print) | LCCN 2022033201 (ebook) |
ISBN 978-0-593-64380-8 (trade) | ISBN 978-0-593-64381-5 (lib. bdg.) |
ISBN 978-0-593-71023-4 (int'l) | ISBN 978-0-593-64382-2 (ebook)
Subjects: CYAC: Flying machines—Fiction. | Secrets—Fiction. | Fossil fuels—Fiction. |
Families—Fiction. | LCGFT: Novels.
Classification: LCC PZ7.D927 Pr 2023 (print) | LCC PZ7.D927 (ebook) |
DDC [Fic]—dc23

The text of this book is set in 12-point Horley Old Style MT Pro.
Interior design by Jen Valero

Printed in the United States of America
1st Printing
First Edition

Random House Children's Books supports the First Amendment
and celebrates the right to read.

Penguin Random House LLC supports copyright. Copyright fuels creativity,
encourages diverse voices, promotes free speech, and creates a vibrant culture.
Thank you for buying an authorized edition of this book and for complying with
copyright laws by not reproducing, scanning, or distributing any part in any
form without permission. You are supporting writers and allowing
Penguin Random House to publish books for every reader.

PROJECT F

PART 1

A Rescue Journey

1

The Terrible Accident

All was going well in our country at the time this story begins, which is several hundred years in the future from the time you're reading it. There were no wars, few wildfires and floods, no famines. Almost everyone lived in one of the seven cities. They were small cities, and all of them were within a two- or at most three-day train ride of each other. They were built as circles, with a center from which the streets radiated out like the spokes of a wheel. If you could have seen them from above, at night, glowing softly with their thousands of lights, brightest in the middle, fading toward the edge, you would have thought they looked like seven golden chrysanthemums scattered over the vast dark land.

Centuries of work had gone into building these cities; it wasn't easy. At any point, there could have been a wrong turn that ruined everything. There still could be. Such a point was approaching, in fact, and its outcome depended (though he didn't know this yet) on a black-haired boy named Keith Arlo, who was at his home in Cliff River City at the moment his parents received a letter.

Margaret Arlo, Keith's mother, opened the letter and read: " 'Dear Mr. and Mrs. Arlo, We are very sorry to inform you . . .' " Her face went pale, and she read on without speaking. She handed the letter to Keith's father, whose name was Arthur. He took the letter, scanned it, and said, "Oh no."

"What is it?" Keith asked.

His father handed him the letter, and he read it quickly. *Unfortunately,* it said, *being unfamiliar with ocean tides and currents . . . did not notice a sudden large wave . . . husband went in to rescue . . . but both were swept away.*

"Swept away?" Keith said. "Does it mean they've drowned?"

"It would seem so," his father said. "Alice and Dennis both."

Keith's mother leaned against the wall, held her hands at the sides of her face, and stared at the air. Alice was her sister; Dennis was Alice's husband.

Keith read on. . . . *as nearest relatives, you will be responsible for the child, left on the beach . . . currently in the care of Sandwater Children's Home.*

"I can't understand this," said Keith's mother.

" 'The child,' " Keith said. "That would be Lulu."

"Let's go and sit down." Keith's father turned away. "This is a shock. We need to think."

They sat talking until late into the night. At first, Keith's mother cried, and his father put an arm around her and tried to comfort her. "I *knew* it was a mistake for them to move," she said between sobs. "Why did they do it? If they hadn't, they'd be here alive right now."

"They wanted something new," said Keith's father sadly. "Warmer weather, different scenes. They were young and adventurous. And a bit foolish."

"I *begged* them not to go," said Keith's mother. "I knew something bad would happen."

"Bad things can happen anywhere," said his father. "You just wanted your sister to keep on living next door."

"True. I did."

After a while, when Keith's mother was a bit calmer, they talked about Lulu, who was six years old. "She must come and live with us," his mother said.

"Yes," said his father. "We'll have to get her back. Right away. Somehow."

Ordinarily, Keith's parents would have made the trip. But his father couldn't leave his business; he was a prominent battery maker in the city, and his shop, full of the wires and metals and fluids that could be put together to produce electricity in small amounts (enough to run a lamp or a fan), was always busy. And his mother, a designer of

5

arches and columns and doorways for the Department of Buildings, had missed a step on a stone staircase the day before and broken her ankle. She could hardly walk.

Keith said right away: "I'll go."

His mother said, "Keith. A thousand misfortunes can happen on a two-day trip, especially to someone like you."

"Four-day trip," said Keith. "Two days each way."

"Curse this foot," said his mother. "I'd be on the train in a minute if I hadn't missed that step."

His father simply said, "It's a big responsibility."

Keith reminded them that he was smart, capable, strong, and almost fourteen years old (though his birthday was not for another eight months).

They talked for a long time. Keith's father kept pulling at his beard, as he often did when he was anxious. But finally he said, "I suppose I could explain what you'd need to know," and from that point, it was decided.

The next morning, Keith and his father left their home on the top floor of the Brightspot Apartments and started down the three flights of stairs. They passed Amity Wing, who was also going down. She was a pretty girl with long dark hair who lived on the second floor with her parents, and when Keith said, "I'm off on a train trip!" she raised her eyebrows and smiled. "Lucky you!" she said. "I've never been, but I'd love to go." Many times, he'd seen her from his window with her pack of friends, all of them talking, laughing, sometimes singing, carrying bags and bundles, heading up the river path. Where did they go? He didn't know. He'd never asked.

Outside, the street was alive with city dwellers and their carts and bikes and wagons, their horses and dogs, their rolling crates of pumpkins, their cages of chickens, their baskets of eggs and pies and mushrooms and flowers. I'm leaving home, Keith said to himself. He had never left home before. It was exhilarating.

They walked down 39th Avenue, beneath the russet-and-yellow leaves of the maple trees, and took the streetcar up Cameron Street to the train station. On platform 2, westbound train #33 stood waiting—engine, fuel car piled high with chunks of wood, and four passenger cars. Steam was already puffing around its wheels. Departure time: 7:30.

"You climb on," said Keith's father. "I want to see you on board and settled."

Keith climbed on. This was his first time on the train, and he found it wonderful: the long row of windows on either side, most of them open to the air; the wood-paneled walls and arched ceiling; and the pairs of seats, cushioned in deep red. His own seat was 12A. He stowed his blue canvas bag in the compartment underneath it, sat down, and thrust the window open. Outside on the platform stood his father, ready to give him parting advice. He was tall, like

Keith, but his shoulders were slightly hunched because he spent so much time bent over his workbench. Keith looked down on him from the window, noticing the strands of white beginning to show in his shaggy dark hair.

"Keep to yourself on this trip," his father said. "Don't get caught up in anything."

"Caught up?"

"You know the way you do."

Keith knew what he meant. Yes, he'd gotten caught up one time in a building project involving stones and water, which had ended badly. Another time, he and a friend had tried to swim the whole width of the river, but the current turned out to be stronger than expected, and they had to be rescued by a fishing boat. The swim was a failure, true, but the *attempt* was brave.

"I won't get caught up in anything," he told his father.

"Remember your mission and stick to it," his father said.

"I will."

The train let out a long hoot and moved forward. Keith waved to his father; his father waved back and then gradually grew smaller and smaller and disappeared.

The conductor came through, collecting tickets. Keith settled back. People chatted or knitted or read or snacked; a child whooped in excitement. At first, there was no passenger in the seat next to Keith's, 12B. This was fine. Keith was outgoing by nature, but he was comfortable with his own company, too. He turned to look out the window.

Beyond the station, at the edge of the city, the train passed storehouses with metal walls, factories of various kinds, big wooden stables, piles of lumber and pipes, stacks of hay, carts loaded with boxes. Keith's uncle—the one who had drowned, Lulu's father—had worked somewhere out here as a craftsman, making chairs and cabinets. Keith thought of him briefly. He'd been a kind, quiet man.

They passed the Western Power Plant, which Keith could see was working at the moment, judging by the thin stream of smoke rising from it. Electricity would be traveling right now across the wires to the places that needed it during the day—the hospital, the streetcars, the telephone wires, certain factories and stores; during the night, electricity was on until eleven o'clock, making the streetlamps and the windows of buildings glow with warm yellow light. (Electricity was one of the Things of Great Value that had been carried forward from the distant past.)

Past the city limits came the fields: cornfields with stalks bleached and broken now that the corn had been harvested, sprawling vines dotted with the last red tomatoes, a vast field of pumpkins and squashes. A path ran alongside the tracks, and sometimes walkers or bikers went by. The train, his father had told him, could go forty-five miles an hour at top speed, so of course no bikers could keep up with it, but some of them tried, pedaling madly. Keith waved at them, and they waved back.

After a while, the passengers' chitchat grew quieter; the only loud sound was the voice of a little girl who walked up and down the aisle, saying "Heh-wo" to each person she passed. It was the kind of thing Lulu would do, Keith thought. Lulu was not a shy little girl.

At 9:46, the train made its first stop, at a shabby station where only one person was waiting on the platform. Hardly anyone lived in the tiny towns way out here; people lived in the cities, and the rest was wild nature, no roads, no paths. Human beings could go there, but only on foot, carrying no tools, making no changes.

Keith twisted around to watch the new passenger come aboard. He was a tall, lanky, long-necked man carrying a blue cloth bag like Keith's and wearing a long-sleeved black shirt. He hurried down the aisle with a quick stride, knocking his bag into the backs of seats and muttering impatiently, tripping over people's feet, grabbing at seatbacks with his big hands. He stopped at the seat next to Keith. "Twelve B," he said. He stooped over and put his bag under the seat. Then he sank down with a great gust of breath. He turned to Keith. He wore glasses, and behind them his eyes were small but keen.

"Are you a talkative type?" he said.

"I can talk or not talk, either way."

"Excellent."

"I'm Keith," he said.

"Malcolm," said the man.

"Is that your first name or your last name?" Keith asked.

"First," Malcolm said. "All you need to know. And you're going where?"

"Sandwater City. What about you?"

"A place called Graves Mountain. Rather remote." Malcolm checked his watch. "I should be there in a little over an hour."

"What will you do at Graves Mountain?"

"I'll be working on an engineering project. Project F, it's called." He smiled slightly, not at Keith, but as if at his own thoughts, some fascinating work he was looking forward to.

"What's it about, Project F?"

"Very complex."

"But I mean—what actually *is* it?"

"I can't go into that."

"Why not?" Keith asked. Curiosity overcame politeness. What did it matter? He'd never see this person again.

A look of irritation passed over Malcolm's face. He swiped at his hair, which was almost long enough in front to get in his eyes. "Some things are not meant for the attention of the general public. At least, not until they're finished."

"Is it almost finished?"

11

Malcolm gave him a thin smile. "It's been great talking," he said. "Now I need a nap. Haven't been getting much sleep lately." He folded out a flap from the side of the seat, and it made a corner he could lean his head into. "See you later." He closed his eyes.

After a while, Keith decided it would be a good time for lunch. Other people clearly thought the same—he heard paper rustling and voices murmuring, and he could smell peanut butter, root beer, and the apples that everyone had this time of year. He reached under the seat, got out his bag, and took from it the packet of food his mother had given him, and the book he'd brought along. He laid out his food on a little table that swung up from beneath the window. The sun shone in; the air smelled like toasted grass. He ate, he watched the world go by, and he felt a pure delight. Of course, not totally pure, he reminded himself, because his mission was a sad one—two people dead, and a child orphaned. But the truth was that at the moment his sadness was slight. He liked being a rescuer; it was, he felt, a job that suited him.

The train rolled smoothly along with a steady, rumbling rhythm. They were going upward now, looping back and forth, rising into the hills and into stretches of forest that grew thicker the farther up they went. Keith checked his watch. It was 10:55. Beside him, Malcolm was sleeping soundly, with his mouth slightly open.

The train slowed. Keith couldn't see anything like

a town, only an opening among the trees. They stopped at a station that looked more like a goat shed—one open room with a hand-drawn sign nailed to its wall: GRAVES MOUNTAIN—the name of the station where Malcolm was getting off. He poked his seatmate's arm. "Malcolm—isn't this your stop?"

Malcolm jolted awake, flashed a look out the window, and jumped to his feet with a swear word. He said, "Thanks, thanks," and with barely a glance at Keith, he stooped to grab his bag and ran down the aisle. Keith watched him hurry away. Lucky I was sitting next to him, he thought. He would have missed his stop.

After that, he read his book for another hour and thirteen minutes. It was a good book, about alien creatures from space, and it helped him fight off afternoon sleepiness. Occasionally freight trains rumbled by on tracks beside the passenger train. They carried everything people might need—lumber, steel, glass, corn flour, wheat flour, sweet potatoes, onions, cranberries, shoes—everything you could think of traveled between the cities on freight trains, mostly but not entirely at night.

Passengers got on and off. Most of them were ordinary people, farmers and shopkeepers, women with children. One person stood out. He boarded at a station called Fieldstone and came down the aisle toward Keith: a big, brown-bearded man in a leather hat with a drooping brim. He wore a thick wool coat with metal buttons, a ragged red cotton scarf around his neck, and great heavy battered-looking boots. He looked rough and bearish, like someone just in from the depths of a forest. Keith stared as the man came clomping down the aisle, and the man noticed him staring, and Keith saw from the squinching of the man's eyes and the slight motion of his mouth-engulfing beard that he was smiling. He took a seat at the back of the car, and later Keith saw him get off at a station called Upper Lake and walk away down the road.

At about seven o'clock, when the sun was on its way down and the train car filled with shadows, there was a stirring and shuffling among the passengers, and the conductor came through calling, "Overnight Inn #49. All passengers off. Train departs in the morning at six a.m. precisely."

Keith got his bag, and he followed the other passengers outside into the chilly darkness. They walked through the station, out a back way, and up a path to the inn, a two-story building with a wide porch and a light glowing above its front door.

Inside, the passengers gathered in a big room lit with lamps and candles. Some shabby old armchairs stood on a frayed carpet. At a long desk sat five travel officers, each with a sign: A THRU F, G THRU K, and so on. Keith stood in the first line, and when he came to the front, he said, "Arlo," and the officer checked him off on a list and handed him

14

a key. "You'll be in room 31," she said. "Upstairs to the right."

Room 31 was small but cozy: one bed, one chair, one tiny table, one lamp with a translucent orange shade. On the wall was a picture of birds flying above a lake. All these Overnight Inns, his father had said, were more or less the same. They were spaced at a distance a train could go in one day; the price of the inn was included in the ticket. The inn stops allowed refueling for the train (there were large woodlots next to every inn) and provided rest for the passengers.

Keith sat down on the bed, set his bag beside him, and opened it.

Something was wrong.

Inside the bag was a black shirt; its front pocket was stitched on with red thread. This was not his shirt. Underneath the shirt was a nightshirt, light blue. It was not his nightshirt. It came to him with terrible clarity what must have happened: he had Malcolm's bag. And even worse: Malcolm had his.

2

Malcolm's Bag

He lifted out the pajamas. Underneath were two pairs of white socks, a blue-and-tan-striped shirt, a pair of black pants, and some underwear. Was it okay to be looking through someone else's things? Maybe not—but maybe there was something in here that said Malcolm's last name and his address. He kept looking.

Some keys on a keyring. A little bag with soap and a razor and a comb. A beaten-up-looking book called *A History of the 21st Century,* by Morton Small. A black sweater with a white lightning bolt on the front. Under all this was a large envelope. There was no writing on it. Keith picked it up and held it flat on his hand. It was heavy, as if it contained quite a few pages. He turned it over. The flap was not sealed. Malcolm's name and address might be in here, so Keith opened the envelope and slid out the pages.

Not writing, as he had expected, but drawings, page after page of them, several drawings to a page. They were done with a fine pen, very complicated, very intricate. What were they? Nothing Keith recognized. They looked like parts of something, maybe a machine. There were a few words here and there, and a few numbers, but they were in such tiny odd handwriting that Keith could make no sense of them. The only words he could read were down at the bottom, in small square print: *Project F.*

It must be the engineering project. Malcolm was designing something, and the drawings were of its parts. Keith put the pages under the lamp and studied them, but the light didn't help. The lines might as well have been meaningless clumps of doodles. And Malcolm's name and address were not written anywhere.

He put everything back in the bag. His mind was spinning. There must be a way he could return all this to its owner and get his own things back, but just then he couldn't think of it.

He slept in his underwear. He was not going to wear Malcolm's nightshirt.

In the morning, he remembered that he'd told his parents he'd call from the inn. He dressed in the same clothes he'd worn yesterday and went downstairs. It was still dark outside. A few travelers were already up, sitting next to their baggage or reading the newspaper or wandering absently around. Keith stopped by the front desk and picked up a rail map, since his old one was gone. He found the telephone in a nook off the lobby and made his call. His father answered. "It's me. I'm fine," Keith said. He had decided not to mention the switched bags; it would just make his parents worry.

"Why didn't you call when you got there?" his father said.

"I forgot. I'll remember from now on."

His mother came on the line and said that they probably shouldn't have let him go alone, and that her foot was killing her, and that she couldn't stop thinking about the family tragedy. "My heart hurts more than my broken ankle," she said. "I can't even work. I have this big project to do, for the power station, and all I can think of is Lulu standing there on the beach, looking out to sea." She sighed. "The poor little thing."

Keith pictured his mother: she'd be sitting at the kitchen table, her hair pulled back and tied with a red string (except for one strand that always came loose), her drawing papers spread out before her. Her project was to design a picture of a rising sun to be carved in stone over the door of Power Station 5, but right now she would not be drawing but staring into the air and drinking cup after cup of orange tea. He could picture his father, too, who would be rushing off to work, hastily eating a piece of toast and getting crumbs in his beard. Keith was sad for a moment. He realized he'd hardly thought of his parents or Lulu at all since yesterday.

"She's being taken care of," he said to his mother. "I'm sure she'll be all right."

Down the hall, he found a little shop called Travelers' Supplies. Clearly, it was meant mainly for people who'd forgotten their toothbrush or soap, but it also had a small selection of clothes. He bought what he needed, including a pair of pajamas with dark green stripes and a traveling bag—red, not blue.

Luckily, he'd had his jacket on yesterday, so he didn't have to buy one of those. Also luckily, he'd had his wallet in his pocket, with the money for the trip and the letter his parents had written to the Children's Home where Lulu was staying. It could have been worse, he thought.

Still, there was the question of what to do about Malcolm's bag. What were those drawings, what was Project F, and why didn't the drawings have explanations? Could it be because Malcolm didn't *want* anyone to know what they were? They could be parts for a bomb, although Malcolm didn't look like a terrorist. Or they could be some invention that would make Malcolm a rich man. Interesting how he hadn't wanted to talk about his work.

Probably Keith should turn the bag in to the Railway Lost & Found, if there was such a thing. But he felt reluctant to do this. He wanted to return the bag himself, with its important papers, and receive astonished gratitude and praise from its owner. He also wanted to hold on to the bag for a while and see if somehow he could make sense of the drawings. A shadow of guilt accompanied these thoughts, but he set it aside.

It was time to get back on the train. Outside, the air was cool, and the sky was cloudy. The travelers walked in a loose, mostly silent crowd the few yards from the inn to the station. The train awaited them, with its headlight beam and its long line of lit windows. Four workers were loading chunks of wood into the fuel car behind the engine. The passengers climbed on and found their seats, and Keith, now carrying two bags, discovered with relief that he had, at least for the time being, no seatmate.

The train moved forward. As soon as it got up to speed, Keith left his seat and wandered through the train until he discovered the snack car, where he bought himself a cinnamon bun, which he brought back with him to his seat. While he ate it, he examined his railway map.

He would reach Sandwater City late this afternoon, spend the night at the Children's Home, and begin the return trip in the early morning. On the way home, the train would pass Graves Mountain. This was his idea: Why not hold on to Malcolm's bag and then stop at Graves Mountain and return it? That would work, wouldn't it? A little adventure that Lulu might enjoy! It would take a bit of extra time, but not much.

He settled in to watch the landscape go by. The clouds grew very dark, and it began to rain. This made the train car seem cozy, as if the travelers were wrapped in a warm, bright, moving cocoon. Raindrops trailed down the windows and sometimes streaked sideways with the wind. Keith saw flashes of lightning to the west, and over the rumbling wheels, he heard a crack of thunder.

Soon the hills were behind them, and they were riding across fields and through forests of trees whose leaves were starting to turn yellow and fall. Grasses bent in the wind, and overhead a flock of blackbirds wheeled and shifted in the sky. Once, in the afternoon, the train slowed and came to a stop. Keith stuck his head out the window, though rain was still falling lightly, to see what was happening. Three bears—a big one and two half-grown cubs—lumbered toward the engine and crossed the tracks in front of it. Keith had not realized that bears were so big—maybe half the size of horses. They seemed to understand that the train would stop for them.

No sign of human presence was in sight in any direction. He had expected this. Except for the few tiny towns, everything outside the seven cities, in the great spaces of land between the rail lines, belonged to the plants and animals. Human beings were just one of the many kinds of earthly creatures; they occupied the space they needed, and that was all. There had been roads and buildings here centuries ago. But when that civilization fell apart, strong stems grew up through the pavement and walls and cracked them, leaves and dust sifted down and turned to earth and buried the roads and broken buildings so deeply hardly a sign was left. Wolves now roamed in some of these places, and so did buffalo and moose and coyotes, and a myriad of smaller creatures: raccoon, skunk, prairie dog, beaver, weasel, fox, mole, mink, mouse, frog, lizard, snake, and bat. And of course the birds in their millions—they could go everywhere: the smallest were the tiny humming-birds, like flying jewels, and the biggest, Keith had heard, was a bird called the condor, with a nine-foot wingspan. It must be, he thought, about big enough for a person to ride on. He imagined himself on the condor's back, grip-ping the stiff black feathers, gazing out over the land below. He opened his window and let in the wind and the scent of earth.

Later in the afternoon, when the sun started sliding down the sky and he grew tired of seeing fields and trees, he pulled out Malcolm's book, *A History of the 21st Cen-tury.* When he opened it, he saw that it had been nearly ruined. Many of its pages had been torn out—violently, it seemed: the edges by the spine were ragged. Some pages re-mained, but nowhere near enough to read the book straight through. He didn't feel like reading it, anyhow.

But he did think for a few minutes about the history he'd learned in school. He knew that three hundred years ago (or was it three hundred and fifty? or maybe five hundred?) his country (or was it the whole world?) had gone through a terrible time and had come out of it only with great effort and determination. One way of life had changed into a different way of life, he knew that. He knew that the old way had been both wonderful and terrible, but he was fuzzy on the details. The wonderful part was that people had miraculous things and could go incredibly fast. There were cars, he remembered that much, in which people could ride long distances, and there were rockets that flew into space. In his imagination, a haze of golden light surrounded the old world, and within it, people lived at the speed of supernatural beings.

The terrible part had something to do with the weather changing. He didn't remember why that had been such a problem. They had solved it, somehow, before it got completely out of control. (But how? He should have paid more attention in history class.) Maybe he'd take a look at Malcolm's book on the train ride home.

At 5:17, the train arrived at the Sandwater station. A man there told Keith how to get to the Children's Home, and since it wasn't far, he decided to walk. He set off down the road, carrying his two bags.

3

Lulu

The buildings here were lighter colors than the ones in Keith's city, and their window frames and balconies were painted red, orange, yellow—all the sun colors. Big trees with pale bark and leaves as big as hands shaded the walkway. To his surprise, the air smelled like salt and pickles.

When he'd walked a few minutes, he came over a rise in the road, and there, beyond a wide strip of sand, was the ocean. Somehow he hadn't grasped that it would be so big. He had to turn his head all the way from side to side to see it. It stretched out to a faint misty line, where it must be spilling over the curve of the planet. He thought of Lulu's parents, who, being ignorant of ocean waves, had drowned here, and that accident suddenly seemed real to him— the deep, cold, enormous water, and the two tiny people waving their arms and legs, struggling against it. He shivered, though the air was warm.

He went on to the Children's Home. It was a big shabby old wooden building, painted white except where the paint had peeled away and left patches of gray. Keith opened the front door.

Inside, he heard children's voices and smelled children's smells—peanut butter, finger paint, rubber toys, a bit of grubbiness. Pinned on the walls were pictures drawn by children in big ragged strokes of bright colors. Keith realized he had not been anywhere near the world of childhood since he himself was a child. It was like a foreign land.

A chubby woman at a desk greeted him. He told her his name.

"Ah! Keith Arlo! Lulu has been so looking forward to your arrival. I'll fetch her." She went off down the hall.

Keith waited, and in a moment, the chubby woman reappeared. Lulu was holding her hand, but when she saw Keith, she broke away and ran toward him.

"There you *are!*" she shouted as she ran. "It took you so *long!* Why didn't you hurry up?" She banged into him, flung her arms around his waist, laid her head against his stomach, and sobbed. "I've been waiting and waiting," she said through her tears.

Keith looked down at the top of her head. Her dark hair was parted in the middle and stuck out in two pigtails, each one tied with a red ribbon. "I came as fast as I could," he said. A wave of grief swept through him. For the first time, he really understood what had happened to her.

"Naturally she's sad and upset," the chubby woman said. "You'll need to be careful with her."

Keith stayed overnight in the guest room, and they left in the morning at 7:30 and walked to the train station. Lulu carried her belongings in a small bag—it was bright yellow, Keith was glad to see, and not likely to get confused with anyone else's. They boarded the #17 eastbound train and found their seats. Lulu took the seat by the window, and when the train whistle blew and the wheels began to clank and rumble, she pushed the window open and waved goodbye, even though no one was there to wave to.

Keith took note of this small sad moment and reminded himself to be especially kind. Still, as the day went on, he saw that it was more of a job than he'd expected, traveling with a six-year-old. Lulu was like two different girls. One of them was excited and rowdy, an explorer, a person with a lot to say. "Keith, look at that! A waterfall! It's so HIGH!" "Keith, did you see those *rabbits*?!" She commented on the passengers, too, in a loud fake whisper. "That lady looks like a frog." "How can that man eat with such a huge mustache?" After a period of energy, she'd switch to wants and complaints. "I'm cold. I don't like those black clouds." "I don't want that sandwich, it tastes bad." "When are we going to get there?" When that happened, Keith would trade places with her, wrap her up in a blanket the train provided, and have a period of peace while she took a nap.

At the Overnight Inn #49, they were assigned a room with two beds. Lulu slept like a rock, but in the morning, for a moment, she didn't know where she was. Keith saw her sit up in bed, look all around, then look at him. Her face twisted as if she were about to cry, but she turned away and looked out the window instead. Brave girl, Keith thought.

He felt a small knot of nervousness in his stomach as they got closer to Graves Mountain. To reassure himself, he held in his mind the picture of how it would go: As soon as they arrived, he would tell someone he was looking for a man named Malcolm who was working on Project F, and surely in a town that tiny they'd know. He'd find Malcolm, who would be delighted to have his bag back, and he'd ask what the drawings were. Malcolm would explain, Keith would be amazed and fascinated, and Lulu would find it all very interesting. They would spend the night in the inn and get back on the train in the morning and continue their journey home. That's how it would go. Why wouldn't it?

In the meantime, Lulu got more and more restless. When he wrapped the blanket around her, she wouldn't sleep. She said she was too bored to sleep. She said she needed another cookie, but then when Keith brought it, she wouldn't eat it. She kicked the back of the seat in front of her, causing the passenger in it to turn around and scowl. Finally, Keith said, "I know what. We'll read."

"I don't like reading," said Lulu.

"Then I'll read to you." Keith decided that his book about aliens might be confusing for Lulu, so he got out Malcom's history book instead and made a game of it. "You open the book to any page," he said. "I'll find the most interesting bit on that page and read it to you."

Clearly, Lulu was not thrilled. "This book is all torn up!" she said. "Probably it's a terrible book." But she flopped it open and put her finger down in the middle of a page. "Here. Read this."

Keith read. " 'At about that time, a treasure was discovered deep in the earth that seemed like magic—and *was* magic, in a way. Of course, anything that works real magic is bound to have a high price.' "

"I don't get it," Lulu said.

Keith thought for a minute. "It means you'll have to pay big for something that seems like magic. Like, for instance: There was a guy who suddenly got a special talent—everything he touched turned to gold. Amazing, right? So great! He touched a chair; it became a golden chair. He touched a penny; it became a gold coin. He touched his fork and spoon; they turned into gold. He could get hugely rich! He was so happy he gave his daughter a big hug. He said, 'We'll be rich forever!' And what happened?"

Lulu looked at him, confused for a second. But she was

quick. Her eyes grew big. "Uh-oh," she said. "His daughter turned to gold."

"That's right."

"And the doctor couldn't fix it?"

"No."

"So he didn't have a daughter anymore."

"No. He had a statue of his daughter."

"He was stupid. He should have known that would happen."

"True. But when people are excited, especially when there's money involved, they don't think too well."

The conductor went through just then, calling, "Next stop, Graves Mountain."

"That's where we're getting off," said Keith.

"We are? Why?"

"We're going to make a quick visit to someone I know. It's right on the way. It won't take long." He pulled their bags out from under the seat and put the book away, and when the train stopped, they got out. Keith checked his watch. It was 3:41.

4

Graves Mountain

The one-room train station, lit dimly by one bulb in the ceiling, was empty except for a spider on the bench and some crunched-up peanut bags on the floor. At least, Keith thought, the peanut bags were a sign of life. They stood looking at them as the train started up and rolled away.

"Is this a real place?" Lulu said. She took hold of Keith's arm.

"Yes," he said. "This is right."

It would be twilight soon. All around the station stood pine trees, like a curved wall. No buildings besides the station, no train schedule behind a panel of glass, no telephone. None of this was what Keith had expected. Those drawings looked so expert, and "Project F" sounded important. He'd thought Graves Mountain would be a small, sleek, thriving town full of people working on advanced, complex projects like Malcolm's, so important they had to be done in a remote location and kept secret. (It was true that Graves Mountain had been a place of industry centuries ago, thriving in its way, but it had also been miserable, a place where people worked hard and lived poorly and often died young, hence the mountain's name. There had been a graveyard here long ago, but the headstones had by now crumbled to dust.)

"We'll look around," Keith said, "and find which way to go. I'll know it when I see it."

They put their bags on the bench—surely there was no need to worry that anyone would take them. Keith walked around the station to the right. Lulu held on to him. "Probably," he said, "we'll come to a road or a signpost."

"I don't like this," Lulu said. "I'm freezing."

"Don't worry," said Keith, who was now quite worried himself. Where was the Overnight Inn? Usually, his father had told him, it was right there by the station, or a short distance away. If they couldn't find it, they'd have to spend the night on the station bench. It would be a hard night—the air was very cold. He pushed away these thoughts.

A few steps later, there it was. He hadn't seen it at first because it was directly behind the station: an opening in the trees.

"Here we go!" Keith exclaimed. "It's a road, or a path."

"But to where?"

"To where we're going. I think so, anyway. Let's get our bags."

They fetched the bags from the station bench and made their way again to the road and in among the dark shadows of the trees.

Keith began suffering from doubt. No one here expected them. He was counting on a person who was almost a complete stranger to welcome him and be glad to get his bag back. But what if it turned out that he and Lulu were a bother, and Malcolm didn't care at all about those drawings? He might say, "You came all the way up here because of those *doodles*?" He'd laugh. Or what if Malcolm wasn't here at all? He might have stopped here briefly and moved on.

They kept tripping over roots and stumbling into ruts. The ground was hard and dry. Once Lulu made a wrong step and fell to her knees, and that started her crying, though she wasn't hurt.

"We're almost there," Keith said. "Don't worry, it's all right." To himself, he was saying something different: This was a completely ridiculous idea. What was I thinking? We're both freezing cold, I'm dragging Lulu into the wilderness, maybe there really is nothing here at all. . . .

They rounded a bend and saw a sign. It was white with large black letters that said PRIVATE PROPERTY. DANGER. KEEP OUT. Just beyond it was a fence, a tall wire fence, not the kind you can climb over. There was a gate in the fence.

It looked like the rest of the fence except that it had strips of metal across it in the shape of an X.

They stepped up to the fence and looked through. They saw a wide field on the other side. It looked as big as a ball field, maybe two.

Several men were out there, way across the field. They were looking up, as if expecting rain, and Keith heard a noise, a roaring buzz. In a moment, something dropped to the ground not far from the men and collapsed. They ran toward it.

"Something fell down," said Lulu. "It's moving."

It was. And it was much bigger than a bird. Probably because of the book he'd been reading, Keith thought instantly of aliens from space. What else would drop suddenly out of the sky?

He stared through the shadows. The fallen creature had a humped back. If only there were light! He glanced upward to see if there might be a spaceship above—

But Lulu wasn't interested. She yanked on Keith's arm. "We have to go find somebody!" she cried. "We have to get in there!" She let go of Keith and flung herself at the gate, grabbing the wire with both hands and shaking it. "We want to come IN!" she yelled, and at the same time, a noise like a fire siren swooped up loud and high. *WEE-ooo, WEE-ooo,* over and over, and Lulu screamed along with it. Keith pulled her away from the fence and held her close, and he stood there, frozen, as the noise went on and went on and then suddenly stopped, and in the silence came the thudding of footsteps and the sounds of voices.

In a moment, on the other side of the fence, three men were shining a light at them so bright that Keith couldn't see their faces.

He called out, though his voice was shaking: "I'm looking for Malcolm!"

He felt the light move to his face, and a voice said, "What?"

"It's me, Keith! From the train!"

"What the blazes are you doing here?"

Keith recognized the voice. "Malcolm! Please let us in!"

A different voice said, "You know these two?"

"Let them in."

Someone tweaked something in a box on a post and rattled some latches, and the gate creaked open. Malcolm rushed forward and grabbed Keith by the shoulder. "What's going on?"

Keith started to speak but discovered his teeth were chattering. "I c-c-came because I w-w-wanted . . ."

"Save it for later," Malcolm said. "Follow us."

They stumbled through the dark, across the field, and through a door into a warm room where a fire was burning in a woodstove. Other people were in there, all of them men, as far as Keith could tell. They were sitting at long tables set with plates. The room smelled like stew and smoke.

Malcolm waved his arms around and called out to people. "Can we get some food here, please? We've got these kids, in from the cold. Yes, right here, thanks, no, I don't know why, give them a chance to get warm."

Bowls of stew and hunks of corn bread were put in front of them, and Keith discovered that he was starving. Lulu ate some, too, but she was still tear-streaked and wary, and she spent a lot of time staring around between spoonfuls. She nudged Keith with her elbow. "What is this place?" she said, looking up at him. "Who are these people?"

Keith couldn't answer. The story was too complicated—the switched bags, the drawings, Project F—and besides, he didn't know where they were himself. "It's okay," he said. "I'll tell you later."

Malcolm pulled up a chair next to Keith. He was wearing a dark shirt with a rumpled collar, and over it a purplish wool jacket. His hair looked as if he'd forgotten to comb it for several days. He took a forkful of the large amount of stew in his bowl. "So, Keith," he said, chewing. "I see you have my bag."

"Yes."

"And I have yours."

"Right."

"So is that why you've come? To get your bag back?"

"Yes," Keith said. "But mainly to give back *your* bag."

"I am grateful," Malcolm said. "I have some important

36

papers in that bag, and I was upset when I saw they were gone."

"I'm sure you were," Keith said. This didn't seem the right time to explain that he'd opened the envelope and looked at the drawings.

"You are an honorable young man," Malcolm said. "You've gone to a lot of trouble, and I must say taken considerable risk, to do the right thing. Who is this that you've brought with you?"

"I'm Lulu," said Lulu. "My parents were . . ." She seemed unable to go on.

"They were swept away in the ocean," Keith said. "She's my cousin, an orphan."

"I see. So Keith is taking you home. Another reason for thinking him a very good sort of person." Malcolm smiled. "You have ended up, however, in a place where you don't belong. You'll have to spend the night, since there's no train until tomorrow. We'll find a place for you to sleep, and after breakfast, we'll send you on your way."

"But I'd like to talk to you before we go," Keith said. "Can we do that? Maybe in the morning? The train doesn't go until nine-forty-four."

"Briefly," Malcolm said. "I will have things to do."

Malcolm got himself another large bowl of stew, and when he had finished eating it, he took them to a cabin a short distance away, where there were two skinny beds with a rickety table between them, and on the table a lamp with a plaid shade.

"I don't understand," said Lulu after Malcolm had gone. "Why did we come all this way just to give this guy his bag?"

"Because, Lulu, something interesting is going on here."

"But what?"

Keith didn't know. If he hadn't seen the drawings, if Malcolm hadn't so mysteriously mentioned Project F, if he hadn't seen, or partly seen, in the dark, the creature falling—from a tree? from the sky?—he might have been content with returning the bag. But he wanted to know more.

So he said, "I can't tell you about it tonight. I'll tell you tomorrow. Get out your toothbrush and wash your face, and let's just go to bed. In the morning, everything will be better."

5

Project F

The next morning, they found their way to the same building where they'd eaten the night before. It looked like an old barn with all the paint worn off, with one wide door at the end and no windows. The roof sagged a bit in the middle. Tall weeds grew around it. It would have looked like an abandoned building except for the trampled paths that led up to it and the line of telephone and power poles with their looping wires that came down the hill behind it.

They went in through a door in the back with a small sign on it. The sign said PROJECT F in hand-painted letters.

Lulu was more cheerful this morning. Being in this odd place still puzzled her, but today it seemed a bit more interesting than scary. "That sign on the door says Project F," she said. "Could F stand for fun?"

"Maybe," Keith said.

"Or maybe family? Or friendly?"

"Could be," said Keith. He smiled, though he was pretty sure Lulu's guesses were wrong.

They found the kitchen by following the breakfast smells to a room at the back. Malcolm was sitting at a big table with several other people. They went to sit with him. He was wearing the same rumpled dark shirt again today; there was a small letter F embroidered on the front in purple. He still hadn't combed his hair, or maybe he'd slept wrong on it—some was sticking out on one side. He looked, Keith thought, like a person too absorbed in important things to waste time with small things.

There were pancakes and scrambled eggs on a plate in the middle of the table.

"Have some," Malcolm said without smiling. He served himself five pancakes and a heap of eggs.

Keith filled his plate and Lulu's.

"I have your bag for you," Malcolm said, pulling Keith's blue bag from under his chair. "I didn't snoop around in it."

Keith felt a bit embarrassed at this, but he thanked Malcolm. He would stuff this bag into his new red one, he thought, so he didn't have to carry two.

"Now," said Malcolm, "what do you want to ask me about?"

Keith felt much better this morning, which made him feel braver. He put last night's terrors behind him; from now on, things would get back on course.

"First, I have to tell you that I looked in that envelope that was in your bag."

Malcolm put down his fork. "You did?"

"Because there was no name or address on your bag. I thought I might find them on the papers in the envelope."

"But you didn't."

"No. But I saw those drawings. I thought they were wonderful. And so intriguing! I couldn't help looking at them. I thought they looked like parts of something. But parts of what? That's what I want to ask you."

Malcolm took a bite of scrambled eggs and chewed slowly. He said, "You're right. They are drawings of a crucial part of the project I've been working on."

"Project F," said Keith. "Those were the only words on those pages that I could read. What *is* Project F?"

"As I said before: I can't tell you that."

Lulu tugged on Keith's sleeve. "I can't eat all these pancakes."

"You don't have to. Just eat what you want." He turned back to Malcolm. "Really? You can't tell me at all? Even just a hint?"

"Very sorry. I'm sure it wouldn't interest you, anyhow. It remains unfinished at this point."

"But now that you have your drawings—will that be sort of the finishing touch?"

"My drawings are an essential improvement. Losing them has delayed us a few days, but that's all."

"Delayed you from what?"

"From launch."

"*Launch!* You mean . . ." Keith lowered his voice. "You mean it's a *rocket?*"

"Of course not. I meant 'launch' as 'introducing something new,' that's all." His plate was empty now. He reached over and took one of Lulu's uneaten pancakes and ate it in three bites. "Curiosity is good," he said, "but it's not so good to look into things that aren't meant for you to know."

Lulu interrupted, leaning across Keith and speaking to Malcolm. "Could a person go in a rocket?"

"We're not building a rocket," Malcolm said.

"I know, but if you were, could a person go in it?"

"No," said Malcolm. He stood up. "Time for you two to get going," he said. "Put your stuff together, and I'll walk you down to the train station."

In the daytime, the forest seemed friendlier. Light glimmered among the trees, and a scent of pine rose from their footsteps. Small birds flew among the branches. It took only about ten minutes to get to the station, which looked just as shabby as it had the night before. "I know there's still a while before the train comes," Malcolm said. "But I'm going to be busy this morning, so it's better for me to say goodbye now. Thank you again, Keith, for making the effort to return my bag. It was thoughtful and brave of you."

"You're welcome," Keith said. "Good luck with your project."

"But what *is* your project?" Lulu said in a loud, frustrated voice.

"It's a secret," Keith told her. "We're not supposed to know."

Malcolm shrugged and smiled at her, as if saying *Sorry, but what can I do?* She scowled at him.

"Have a good trip," Malcolm said. He took a few steps backward, clearly in a hurry to get away.

"We will." Keith set his bag and Lulu's on the bench and sat down. "Bye."

Malcolm turned away and took off toward the path in long strides.

"Okay, Lulu," Keith said when he was gone. "It is now"—he checked his watch—"eight-thirty-six. The train gets here at nine-forty-four. That means we have about an hour."

"Just to sit here and wait?"

"That's not what we're going to do. We want to see what Malcolm's project is, right?"

"Right."

"I have a plan. We stay here for a while, long enough so they'll all be finished with breakfast and out working. Then we go back through the woods, we hide among the trees, and we watch."

Lulu's eyes went wide.

"Want to do that?" Keith asked.

She nodded, smiling a little smile.

43

"Good. We'll go in about fifteen minutes."

They sat. Lulu swung her feet back and forth. After a few minutes, she said, "Read me something out of that torn-up book."

"Okay." Keith still had the book, because he'd accidentally put it in his own bag (the new red one he'd bought) instead of Malcolm's the night before, when he was reading to Lulu on the train. He hadn't meant to, and Malcolm hadn't seemed to notice that it wasn't there. So Keith had kept it. He could always mail it back after he got home.

He took it out and let Lulu open it. She pointed to a page. "Read from here."

Keith read:

> With the powerful energy they had harnessed, human beings built a more and more complex way of life. By the late 20th century, most of the countries of the world lit their cities with electricity; nearly all the people of the world had cars to carry them from place to place; airplanes flew people through the sky, and huge ships crossed the oceans, trading goods between people in every country.

"I don't want to hear about oceans," Lulu said. "Turn some pages."

Keith turned some pages and read:

> *By then, everything depended so completely on this kind of energy—that is, energy from burning coal, oil, and gas, which were called fossil fuels—that when a storm or an accident caused the power to go out, even for just a few days, things started to fall apart. Lights went dark in whole cities, elevators got stuck on high floors, subways came to a stop, trucks couldn't deliver food and other goods to stores. If it was winter, heaters went off, and it was too cold; if it was summer, air coolers went off, and it was too hot.*

"But were people more silly back then?" Lulu said. "Power goes out in our city all the time, and those bad things don't happen. We just wait, and it comes back on."

"Maybe," Keith said, "the more wonderful your life is, the more terrible you feel when it goes wrong."

"But why *would* it go wrong?"

Keith had no answer for this.

"And what's an elevator? And a subway?" Lulu asked.

"I don't know." Keith checked his watch and closed the book. "It's time to go. We can put our bags under the bench. We'll find a good place to hide, and if we're lucky, we might see something."

They made their way through the woods. The trees were so close together that in some places their branches intertwined. Keith pushed them upward so there was room to stoop underneath. Brown leaves showered down around them. After several minutes, Keith spotted a wide tree trunk surrounded by dense bushes. Beyond it was the fence. They crept behind the trunk, and he held the brushy branches apart to make a space they could both see through.

They had a clear view of the field. They waited. Then, from a large shed at the end of the field, several men came out. Malcolm was not among them. Each one was carrying an armful of equipment—hoses, cylinders, cables, straps, packets—things that didn't add up, in Keith's mind, to anything in particular. The men set these things down on the ground in a careful, orderly way. They were talking; Keith could hear their voices but could not make out what they said.

Lulu spoke into Keith's ear in a loud whisper: "What are they doing?"

"Just watch," Keith whispered back. "And be *quiet*. Don't say *anything*." He knew they must make no noise, not even the sound of one twig tapping against another.

A different man came out now and joined the ones on the field. He was a tall, muscular man, wearing a blue suit that fit him tightly, like a skin. Some cheerful greetings passed among the men; a couple of them gave the man in blue a thump on the back. Then they began loading him with the equipment they'd laid on the ground. They strapped a pack to his back, tubes to his arms, bundles of something to his ankles, and coils around his waist, and they settled a round helmet on his head. The man stood still for all this, like a statue, with his arms angled slightly away from his body.

The other men stepped aside. No one moved for a moment. Keith heard one voice calling a question. The man in blue answered. He moved his arm in and did something near his waist that Keith couldn't see. Then came a rushing sound, very loud, and wisps of flame shot out from the man's feet and behind his back, and the man himself began to rise into the air.

Lulu gasped. Keith clapped a hand over her mouth. They both stared as the man went higher, tipped forward, spread his arms, and flew. He wasn't as high as the treetops, and he didn't fly far. After just a minute or so, he sloped downward and landed, tumbling over in a heap. All the other men ran toward him, which brought them closer to Keith and Lulu's hiding place than they had been before.

Again, they watched as the man in blue was checked over and adjusted. Again came the whoosh and the flames, and again the man rose into the air with a rushing, roaring noise. This time, he kept on going, at a steep slant, until he was higher than the trees. He turned in the air and sailed smoothly for a moment, so high that his blue suit almost disappeared against the sky. Then came a sputtering sound, and the man aimed himself steeply down toward the ground and landed with a thump. His knees buckled, and he fell. The men ran toward him, shouting, "Okay? Are you okay?" but the flier waved them away and got to his feet and grinned. He said, "Next time for sure," and then the other men surrounded him.

Keith made no sound, but his mind was blazing. A person can fly! he thought. I could fly. I want to. Everybody will want to.

6

Inside Information

Keith took Lulu by the hand. He raised a finger of the other hand in the "quiet" sign and began stepping backward out of the shadow of the big tree, and then turning around to go back the way they'd come. He went at a snail's pace, checking the ground for things that might trip them or make a crackle, and at the same time, his mind raced. Imagine a world where people could fly! The Graves Mountain team hadn't perfected their machine yet—but they would. And he had gotten a preview. He could tell people what he'd seen, help get them excited and eager for the new way of things. He could—

That was the moment when Lulu stumbled, stamped hard on a branch that broke with a loud crack, and fell to the ground, pulling him down as well. She must have landed on something sharp—she cried, "O-o-ow!" and it came out as a howl.

From the field, someone said, "Wait! Did you hear that? Someone's in there!"

"Are you hurt?" Keith whispered. Lulu shook her head.

They struggled to stand, but branches cracked again, and again both of them stumbled and fell. A voice cried, "Over there! Outside the fence!" Running footsteps sounded, and a moment later, the gate creaked, someone crashed toward them, and a man with a red beard appeared between two trees.

"It's the kids!" he yelled, and the other men came up behind him. They looked down at Keith and Lulu, crumpled on the ground amid the sticks and the dirt, and Keith felt stupid and afraid.

"They're the ones Malcolm brought in last night," said the man with the beard. He pointed down at Keith. "Come on," he said. "Malcolm is going to want to talk to you."

Keith and Lulu scrambled up from the ground. They followed the men, edging between the trees, stepping over rocks and branches, and they crossed the field, going toward one of the buildings, where they went in through the front door. "Malcolm!" the bearded man yelled. "Are you here? Look what we found!"

They were in a hallway with stairs to the right and a large room to the left, a workshop of some kind, with tall machines and metal cabinets and tools and devices Keith couldn't identify. Malcolm was in there, hunched over a drafting board. When he heard Red Beard's voice, he whirled around and stared at them with his mouth open. "Oh, rats from hell," he said. "What happened?"

"They were spying," said Red Beard. "From the woods." He led Keith and Lulu into the workshop.

"I wanted to see what you were building," Keith said. "I couldn't help it! My curiosity was too strong! And now that I've seen it, I know it's a thing of genius!"

At that moment, the long wail of the train whistle sounded.

It was the train they should have been on. Everyone stood still and listened. Keith heard the wheels going more and more slowly, then speeding up again. No passengers at the station, no need to stop.

"I have blood on me," said Lulu, wiping a scratch on her arm.

Malcolm glared at them. "This is not what we need," he said.

"Not at all," said Red Beard.

"But listen," Keith said urgently. "It's only for a day. We'll take the train tomorrow. Today I can help you!"

"Ha."

"Really! I can—I want to! I can tighten screws or polish metal or oil joints or—"

"Out of the question," Malcolm said. His voice trembled with rage. "This is a complex, highly classified operation. You have no idea what you've gotten yourself into."

"You could tell me," Keith suggested. "Since we've seen it anyhow. Otherwise, we might go home and say all the wrong things about it."

"You must say *nothing* about it!" Malcolm shook a finger at them, and his face went red.

"It would be better," Keith said, "if you'd explain to me why it's so important and why it has to be a secret. I'm pretty good at keeping secrets, if I know why I'm keeping them." An idea came to him, along with a sly, tingling feeling of power. "If I don't know," he said, "I might think you're making something evil. I might tell people that."

Red Beard was standing by, listening. He stepped up to Malcolm and whispered in his ear. Malcolm frowned and brushed him away. But Red Beard persisted. Keith couldn't hear what he was saying, but he could tell that Malcolm was now listening. He directed a piercing stare at Keith.

"All right," Malcolm said. "I'll explain a few things to you, you can hang around today without interfering, and before you leave, *both* of you will sign a promise to say nothing of what you've learned."

Keith agreed to this.

"You mean even me?" said Lulu.

"Even you."

Red Beard left, closing the door behind him. Malcolm dragged out a couple of stools. "Sit there." He turned his own chair from his drawing board to face them and leaned forward with his hands on his knees. "First of all, you should know the magnitude of this operation. We are not building a toy here, or a museum piece. We have only one draft of our product right now, our Model F, almost completed, but we are looking toward massive production, and we have backing from powerful sources. Have you heard of Firebrand Fiber? And Lightspeed Power?"

"Yes," Keith said. He had a vague memory of hearing those names.

"They are behind us, and so are others, just as big."

"Behind you?" Lulu bent sideways, trying to see behind Malcolm.

"It means money," Keith told her. "Those companies are giving money to the project."

"Right," said Malcolm. "They know it will change the world." He gave Keith a sharp look. "I sense that you understand this."

"I think so," Keith said. "It's because anybody could have one, and anybody could go anywhere."

"That's right. Think how vast this country is, with all its unreachable spaces. With the Model F, those spaces could be *made* reachable."

To Lulu, this was a boring conversation. She got up and wandered over to a tall cabinet and began pulling open each of its drawers.

"Don't *do* that," Malcolm said to her.

Lulu turned around. "Why not?" she said. "They're just papers. I can't understand them, anyway."

"Don't be mad at her," Keith said. "Let her look around. She won't hurt anything. It might be better if she *doesn't* listen to what you say."

Malcolm made a grumpy sound, but he didn't say any more to Lulu.

"So why does the Model F have to be secret?" Keith asked. "Why not get the world all excited about it before it's done, and then when it comes out, they'd be lining up to buy it?"

"Listen," Malcolm said. "If we let people know what we're doing, there are some who would try to stop us. To chop us at the root, so to speak, before we can really take off."

"But why?"

Malcolm sat back and sighed impatiently. "To keep things *the same*, Keith. The powerful people want every-thing to remain the same, as it has for so long. They have squashed ideas like ours over and over. But they can't squash something they don't know about."

Keith still wasn't sure what it was about the Model F that powerful people would want to squash, but Malcolm was making him feel slightly stupid, as if he *should* know this but didn't.

Malcolm leaned forward. He aimed the beam of his small piercing eyes straight at Keith. "We want to bring something new to our country, something terribly important. Can you guess what it is?"

"It must be what the F stands for in Model F, and Project F," Keith said. "Is it flight?"

"That's one thing, yes. But the great thing is freedom. The Model F will bring *freedom* to this country, for the first time in hundreds of years." He gazed fiercely into the air, as if he were already seeing the glories to come.

Lulu was over at Malcolm's drawing board by now, peering at the sheets of paper on it. She wasn't quite tall enough to see, so she took a book down from a nearby shelf and stood on it. Malcolm whirled around. "Quit that!" he said. "Don't you *know* not to touch other people's things?" He turned to Keith. "That's all for now. Please get your little sister under control."

"I'm his cousin, not his sister!" Lulu shouted. "Don't you *listen* to what other people say?"

Keith thought it best to end the conversation, though he had many more questions. "We'll let you get back to your work," he said, turning toward the door.

"Wait," Malcolm said. "I'd like to give you a glimpse of just how complex and powerful this operation is. You'll understand what you've got yourself into. Come this way."

Keith followed him out into the hall.

Malcolm beckoned to Lulu. "You too. I don't want you poking around in my office."

He led them to a door at the far end of the hall. There was a lock on its latch, which he opened with a key, and they went through into a wider passage with doors all along it, and cold as a cave. In fact, Keith thought, it probably was a cave, but a man-made cave, dug into the hill in back of the few buildings visible from the outside. Anyone who might be hiking around in these woods (extremely unlikely) and happened upon this clearing would have no way to know that it wasn't just a half-abandoned old camp, with its few shabby buildings and littered playing field. They wouldn't know that one of the buildings opened into this underground place.

Pipes and cables ran along the ceiling, and at infrequent intervals, a light bulb gave a dim glow. They passed a huge room that looked to be full of wooden crates, stacked one on top of another, and beyond that another huge room, also full of stacked crates.

"What's in all those boxes?" Lulu asked.

"Nothing you need to know about," Malcolm said.

At the end of the passage was a double door, closed. On the wall above these doors was the only thing of beauty Keith had seen here so far: a painting of the letter F, done in blue, purple, and white, drawn in swooping curved lines, slanted forward, as if the F were about to fly away.

"What's behind those doors?" Lulu wanted to know.

"We won't be going in there," said Malcolm.

But Keith heard a sound from behind the doors, a clacking sound like wheels on a track, and a clatter, like the dropping of a load of rocks. He didn't know what this might be, and it was clear that Malcolm wasn't saying.

He heard another sound, too, as Malcolm led them down still another passage. It was a deep, steady thumping sound, as if a giant with huge feet were stamping over and over again. He couldn't tell where it was coming from. "What's that thumping?" he asked Malcolm.

"Part of the refining process," Malcolm said. "It takes place way at the back."

They came around to where they'd started. "So you see," he said when they were out in the field again, "this is not a trivial operation."

Keith understood. Huge amounts of work and money had gone into this. Clearly, the people doing it were determined to succeed in a big way. "I find it extremely exciting," Keith said. "And inspiring."

Malcolm looked at him with true interest for the first time. "Smart boy," he said. "I think you're getting it."

"One more question," Keith said. "The Model F makes flames. What kind of fuel is it burning?"

"Nothing you would have heard of."

"But does it have a name?"

"It's called . . ." Malcolm paused and cleared his throat with a loud raspy sound. "It's called . . . black dust."

"You're right, I've never heard of it. It's not a kind of electricity?"

"No, no. Something entirely different."

"So that's the key to it, then—very powerful fuel."

"That's right—and clever engineering. Remember," he said, "not a word to anyone. Or there will be—let's just say consequences."

"I know." Keith meant what he said. He would keep the secret, though he knew it would be hard.

"I'll be consulting with my crew this afternoon," Malcolm said. "We may have something more to talk to you about. Meet me right here"—they were at the edge of the field, by a crooked tree—"at one o'clock."

And of course Keith said he would.

7

Up in the Air

Back in the cabin, Keith stood by the window looking up the hill, his mind teeming with what he'd seen and heard. He could tell that Malcolm was starting to understand him—to see how quick-witted he was, and how ready to jump at a new adventure. He'd been so right to take the chance of coming here.

He knew he'd gotten "caught up" in something, as his father had warned him not to. But it was okay, because it was such an astounding chance, how could he have said no to it? Surely even someone as stodgy as his father would have wanted to fly. Still, he knew both his parents would be furious at what he'd done. He had put himself in danger, and possibly Lulu, too. But no harm had come to them! And anyhow, his parents would never know because he'd never tell them. In a year or two, when flying machines were everywhere, he could tell them that he had known about it from the first. They would be amazed.

Before they went out to the field, Keith used the telephone in Malcolm's office to call home. His father answered. "About time," he said. "We thought you'd be home yesterday. When we didn't hear from you, we were quite worried."

"I'm sorry. Things got busy."

"But you'll be home this afternoon, right?"

"No, tomorrow."

"Tomorrow?! Is there a problem? What's going on?" Keith could hear the fear and anger in his father's voice.

"Nothing, Father. I'm fine. So is Lulu. I'll tell you all about it when we get back. See you soon!" He hung up, feeling a pang of guilt, which he quickly swept aside.

A little before one o'clock, Keith went out to the train station to get their bags, taking Red Beard with him to open the gate. Then he and Lulu met Malcolm by the crooked tree. The five men of his crew were with him.

"All right, everyone," Malcolm said. He spoke sternly and stood very straight, with his hands on his hips, like a general. "As you know, we have a situation. We've had what you might call a security breach from an unexpected direction: these two." He pointed at Keith and Lulu. "I've talked with some of you already. I think you all know what I'm proposing."

Lulu interrupted loudly. "I'm the only girl here! How come nobody else in this place is a girl?"

"Interesting question," said Malcolm, "but not the one we're here to address. We're speaking of important things right now. Interruptions are not helpful." He turned to Keith. "How much do you weigh, young man?"

"A hundred and ten pounds," said Keith, who was tall but quite slim.

"About right," Red Beard said.

"And are you an athletic sort of person?"

"Definitely. Champion at soccer, and I ride my bike at top speeds."

"Pretty strong, then?"

"Oh, yes. I'm much stronger than I look."

Malcolm faced his team. "You all know where I'm going with this. How many agree?"

They agreed, all but one, a man with a pinched face and wispy brown hair. "What if . . . you know, an un-fortunate . . . which probably wouldn't happen, but . . ." He trailed off.

"Of course we've considered that," said Malcolm. "I can assure you it wouldn't happen."

"How can you know?"

"An EP-1 pack will be included."

The pinch-faced man nodded. "All right."

"What I want to know," said Red Beard, "is how we're

expecting to keep this one quiet once they go back home." He pointed at Lulu.

"It won't matter," Malcolm said, "because she doesn't understand. She can describe what she saw, but she won't be believed."

Lulu was insulted by this. "I'm good at describing things," she said hotly. "You'll find out."

Keith was listening to Malcolm with complete understanding and rising excitement: they were going to let him fly. Someone less heavy than the man who'd gone up this morning would be easier for the Model F to lift. And a boy in the air, flying free as a bird, would be just the thing to make other people want to fly, too.

He turned to look at Malcolm, who was looking at him with his eyebrows raised. "Are you willing?" Malcolm asked.

"Yes," said Keith, and his heart leapt up and beat *tap-tap-tap* like a hammer.

They walked out onto the field, along a path trodden through the scrubby dry weeds to a space in the middle that had been cleared and raked smooth. The five men came along, one of them pulling a cart carrying the parts of the flying machine.

"This is our team," Malcolm said. "These two are my right-hand guys." He pointed at the man with the red beard and the man standing next to him, who had no beard but the same red hair. "The Stanley brothers, Dodge and

Roam," said Malcolm. "They know everything about this operation."

"We've been with him from the start," said Dodge, who had a broad chest and hairy arms.

"From the start," echoed his brother, a skinnier version of Dodge.

Malcolm went on. "This one is Armando." He pointed to a stout man with heavy black eyebrows. "Next to him is Hugo"—he was muscular and bald and wore sunglasses, and Keith recognized him as the man they'd seen flying— "and this is Sidney." He was the one with the thin hair and pinched face.

Dodge stepped forward and gave instructions in a dramatic voice. "Keith!" he said. "You are about to do something almost no one has done before. It is your great good luck! You may even become famous someday as a result!" He beamed a smile through his rusty whiskers. "Before we begin," he said, taking some papers from a folder he carried, "we'd like your signature on this page, right here, and your address." He handed Keith a pen, held the paper against the folder, and pointed a finger at the line at the bottom.

"What is it?" Keith asked, taking the pen.

"It details the precautions we have taken against any accident and says you have heard them and understand."

"I haven't heard them," Keith said.

"You will, in just a moment."

Keith waited, holding the pen, but Dodge didn't explain, just tapped his finger on the signature line.

Keith was impatient to fly. "I can read it myself later, right?" he said.

"Of course," said Dodge.

So Keith, feeling only very slightly uneasy, signed his name and wrote his address.

"You sign, too," Dodge said to Lulu. "Your signature says you will not tell anybody what you've seen. No one."

Lulu frowned. She was already carrying a secret, one she would probably never tell. Would it be all right to have two? She was confused and didn't like the feeling. "Nobody explains anything to me," she said. "I don't even know what's on that piece of paper."

"It's all right," Keith said. "It just means you know I'm going to fly."

She could tell that he really, really wanted to. "So I should sign it?"

"Yes," he said.

She took the pen and printed her name.

Dodge slipped the paper back in the folder. "You might think that going up in the air is dangerous," he said. "It is, slightly. But you will have on your back what's called an EP-1 pack, designed to protect you. In all the times we've used it, it has not once failed."

Probably, Keith thought, it was a parachute. He knew

about them. Some people, for sport, went up on high cliffs at the edge of the city and jumped off wearing parachutes, for the fun of floating down. This sounded fine to Keith.

"If today's flight goes well," Dodge continued, "we may have a special request for you later. All right?"

"Sure."

"Good. Let's go, then."

Dodge and Armando picked up the parts of the machine from the cart. They lowered a frame of lightweight metal over Keith's shoulders and fastened it with a thick belt around his waist. In the front, two upright handles stuck out from the frame. "You will hold on to these," said Dodge, "and move them to go left or right." Keith gripped them. They were like the handles on a bike. He pulled to the right; he pulled to the left. Easy.

Armando knelt behind him and fastened a tube to the back of each of his legs. "These are power tubes," he said. "They will burn very hot, but the flames won't touch you; they'll go past your heels and down. Hold your arms out." Keith did. Armando and Dodge attached a kind of flap to each arm. "These are for horizontality," Dodge said. "Don't worry, you'll get to practice all this."

Keith said he wasn't worried, which was true.

Last came a pack on his back, heavy, like two dictionaries. "This also is propellant," said Dodge. "Two rockets. They are the most powerful and will keep you in the air.

This button here"—he pointed to it on a panel that ran between the handles—"will start the power. This dial adjusts the power. More power, you go up. Less, you descend."

They practiced, without turning anything on.

"Take off," said Armando.

"Starter button," said Keith.

"Increase speed."

"Turn the dial right."

"Go right and left."

"Use the handles."

"Descend."

"Turn the dial all the way left. Slowly."

They did this several times, until Keith was adept at quickly finding the right thing to press or turn.

"You can do it?" Armando asked.

"I'm sure I can."

Malcolm had been watching all this. "He's got it," he said. "Let's go. Keith—onward and upward!"

Keith pressed the power button.

First came a roar, then a steady spitting and hissing, as shafts of flame pressed downward, forcing the ground away, lifting Keith's heels and then his toes. He was in the air, going up. The rockets were hot against his back and his legs. With one hand, he held the left handle, and with the other, he turned the dial. More crackling roar. Higher and higher. Below, he saw the men's faces turned up toward him and the trees like a carpet of spikes. He pressed to the right, leaned in the air, turned. Wind riffled his hair. He pedaled his legs. He spread his arms and the flaps unfolded, and he felt how he could move slightly and they would tip him forward, into a swimming position. The engines roared.

"Higher!" cried someone from below. He heard another voice, too, a high voice, either a cheer or a scream.

He turned the power dial and headed up, higher than the treetops now. Everything below was far away. Around was only sky. It was terrifying and thrilling at once. To be disconnected from the earth! Like this, he could go anywhere. He went left, he swooped down and rose again, he flew to the end of the field, turned around, and flew back. When he was over the team, he heard someone call, "Come down now!" and though he wasn't ready to, he turned the dial and sloped toward the ground and came in easily, almost without stumbling, just running a few steps and then coming to a stop.

Everyone cheered and clapped. Lulu ran up to Keith shouting, "I saw you! YOU FLEW!"

Malcolm said, "Well done!" and looked down upon him with a true smile.

Keith burned with glory. It was like fire in his veins.

One more night in the cabin. Lulu worked on a jigsaw puzzle made of wood that a member of the crew had given her. She was tired and crabby. "This piece won't go in!" she said, pressing her thumb hard on a puzzle piece with her elbow sticking up.

"It must be in the wrong place." Keith got up and helped her until the puzzle was complete. It was a picture of a blackbird perched on a fencepost and a flock of blackbirds in the air. Like me, Keith thought. I'm a new kind of bird.

Lulu flopped down on one of the beds and pressed her face against the pillow. "I'm sick of being here," she said in a muffled voice. "I want to go home." Then her shoulders moved up and down, and Keith could see she was crying. He sat by her and carefully put a hand on her arm.

She shrugged his hand away.

Keith wasn't sure what to do. "How can I help?" he asked. "Do you want to talk . . . to talk about what happened to your—"

"No!" Lulu twisted around with a look of fury and punched his leg, hard. "No, no, no, don't talk to me!" She hid her face in the pillow again.

So Keith let her alone. "Don't worry," he said. "We'll be going home tomorrow."

"Right now, right now!" Lulu's words were blurry with tears. She cried for a long time.

PART 2

At the Brightspot Apartments

8

Not Quite the Truth

They left the next morning. It rained most of the day and was just clearing up as they arrived home, midafternoon. Before they got off the train, Keith reminded Lulu, "We won't say anything about what happened at Graves Mountain, remember? I won't, and you won't."

"I know," Lulu said. She frowned, not looking at him. "I understand about secrets. You can't tell them."

Keith's parents were at the station. His mother was wearing a gray stocking over her bandaged foot, and she was propping herself up with crutches. His father had a woolly plaid scarf around his neck. Its fringed ends flapped in the wind. Both of them looked anxious until they saw Keith and Lulu waving from the window, and their faces lit up, and they waved and came forward, and when their son and their orphaned niece stepped down from the train, they threw their arms wide for a hug. Keith's mother, in her eagerness, stumbled a bit, but his father caught her.

"Hello, Aunt Meg," Lulu said. "Hello, Uncle Arthur." It was strange to think that her aunt and uncle were now her parents.

"Hello, darling Lulu!" said Aunt Meg. She flung out one arm, her crutch fell sideways, and she folded Lulu into a big, one-armed hug. This made Lulu feel both happy and sad. She had to squeeze some tears back into her eyes.

They rode home on a donkey taxi, an open platform with benches on each side, a railing around them, and a yellow canvas top. The city seemed as bright as if it were new, though it was in fact over three hundred years old. You could see this in the paving stones of the streets, worn to shallow dips by thousands of wheels and footsteps, and the scratches and cracks and rain streaks on walls and columns. It was an old but sturdy city, and its age only made it more beautiful.

They rode down Station Street, across 29th Circle, 28th Circle, 27th Circle, and so on until they got to the corner of 19th Circle, where they got off the taxi and walked two blocks down Gannet Street to the Blue Striped Gate, and through it into the courtyard of the Brightspot Apartments, where they lived. The wind was blowing leaves off the courtyard trees and skidding them across the ground; drying clothes whipped back and forth on a clothesline. A woman called out greetings to the family, and a few chickens ran around, and a brown dog slept in a patch of sun.

The Brightspot was a large building, L-shaped, and four stories high, one household per floor. Another building of the same shape was opposite, so walls and windows, walkways and arches surrounded the courtyard on all sides. Like most buildings in the city (except the ones made of stone), these were built from large earth-colored bricks, now so old their edges were worn away, giving the thick walls a soft look, no sharp corners. Windows, framed in wood, faced east, west, or south to catch the sun.

Keith looked up to his own windows and saw them wide open, with the yellow curtains flying out in the breeze. He found himself unexpectedly glad to be home. It was good to be in a familiar place, after so many days of places new and strange. In his building, he knew everyone. On the first floor lived old Gloria Garden, always smiling her gap-toothed smile when she caught you going by, reaching out to grab your shirt and keep you there so she could talk and talk to you. Luckily, she didn't appear today. On the second floor were the Wings, Calvin and Lea, and their daughter, Amity. The third-floor apartment, which had been the home of Lulu and her parents, was empty. When they went past that apartment, Lulu started toward the door, and Keith's mother had to say, "No, no, darling, you live upstairs now." Lulu veered away quickly. She said nothing, but Keith saw her frown and tighten her mouth.

When they reached the top-floor apartment, they were home. Afternoon light streamed into the room from the western windows, and to the east lay the rooftops of the city. In the distance were the windmills, and then the river, like a silver ribbon.

"Now, Lulu," said Keith's mother, "I'll show you your room." She took Lulu's hand and led her to what used to be a sewing room. The sewing things were gone, and instead there was a pink-and-yellow rag rug, and on it a bed with a white cover, a chest of drawers, and a small table and a chair. On the table stood a glass jar holding four peach-colored chrysanthemums. "Do you like it?"

Lulu nodded.

In the main room, they sat down at the table to talk. At first, the parents asked questions of Lulu—*Did you have a good train trip? Did Keith take care of you well? We are so sad about your parents, but we're happy that you'll be with us now.* Lulu didn't say much in return. She looked around, taking in her new home: rug on the floor striped in green and blue, two fat green armchairs, white wooden chairs around the table. Two electric lamps, and in different places around the room, at least a dozen candles in their candlesticks, all different colors, ready for times when the nighttime power went dim or went out. The tall windows that looked east, south, and west were set deep into the walls, so they all had window seats, and the window seats had cushions. In sunny weather, there would be light in the apartment all day; Lulu knew this, because apartment 3 had been the same.

Keith's father, setting down his teacup, said, "All right, then," in a way that meant it was time to get serious. "We want to know, of course, Keith, why you were two days late getting home."

Keith had known this question was coming and had worked hard to find an answer that wasn't quite a lie. "There was a problem on the train," he said. "Something to do with a switch." This was true: his bag and Malcolm's had been switched, and that had been a problem.

"You mean they had to stop for repairs?" his father asked.

Without answering, Keith went on. "And then it rained and rained, and we had to spend the night at an inn." This was also true: it had rained, and they did spend nights at inns, though not because of the rain.

"Ah," said his father. "Which inn?"

"We were at Graves Mountain," Keith said. Also true: they were there, although not at an inn.

Keith was aware that he was not telling his father the truth at all. Lulu was giving him a long steady look. But he was pulled in two directions—don't lie to your father, and at the same time keep the secret of Graves Mountain and the promise on the paper he had signed. It was difficult. He would like to have told his father—and his friends— about the amazing things happening to him, but of course he wouldn't. The secret was like a small warm stone inside him. It felt good.

Keith's father got up to set a fire in the little iron stove. Keith watched through the stove's glass door as the flames caught the edges of the crunched-up paper and began to singe the sticks of wood.

"Father," he said. "Do you know what black dust is?"

His father turned and stood with his back to the stove, warming his legs. "Black dust? I suppose there can be all colors of dust, depending on what the dust came from. Rub a brick, for instance, and you'd get brick-colored dust."

"But what would you rub to get black dust?"

"You could get black dust from a piece of burned wood. You could get it from coal, which of course we do not use. But why would you want it?"

"I don't," said Keith. "I just heard someone talking about it somewhere. Maybe it's a spice."

"Ah, that could be. Finely ground pepper, perhaps."

"That must be it."

For the rest of the evening, as he ate dinner, helped with the dishes, got ready for bed, Keith thought about that one phrase: ". . . which of course we do not use." He wasn't sure what coal was, besides a black sort of stone. What was it for? Why did people not use it? Was black dust made from coal? He couldn't ask his father without telling why he wanted to know. He'd have to find out on his own.

For the next few days, Lulu didn't say much of anything. She looked out the window a lot. She took naps. She was polite. On the third day, she asked Keith's mother—who was Aunt Meg to her—if she could go down and see apartment 3, where she used to live. "You know," Aunt Meg said, "nothing is there anymore." Lulu said she knew but she still wanted to see. So they went down, and Lulu walked around the vacant, echoing rooms for a minute or two. "It looks all different," she said, and that was the last time she wanted to go.

Monday afternoon, Keith stayed after school to talk to his history teacher, Ms. Proger. He found her in her classroom, putting on her coat, getting ready to leave. He said, "May I ask you a question?"

She was surprised, he could tell. He'd never come to ask questions before.

"All right. Have a seat." She sat at her desk, and Keith sat in the front row.

"There are some things I've read about," Keith said. "I want to know if they're true."

Ms. Proger was rather old, perhaps forty, and her hair was short and held tight to her head. She always wore a gray or brown dress with a leaf-shaped pin on the collar. She didn't often smile. "Go on," she said.

"Do you know what black dust is?"

"Black dust?" She looked at him suspiciously. "No. Never heard of it."

"It's a kind of fuel," Keith said.

She frowned at him and leaned back with her chin tucked in, as if he had said something disgusting. "Why do you ask, Keith? Why would you want to know that sort of thing?"

"I saw a mention of it somewhere. Do you know what it is?"

"Possibly. If you're referring to what I think you are, then you may remember I covered it briefly in class—the time of the Sudden Rise and the Sudden Fall. You may have been dozing at the time, Keith, or lost in your imagi-nation. I believe it's most important to learn the history of what has brought the human race together in the last few centuries rather than what nearly destroyed it longer ago than that."

"But then, what exactly—" said Keith.

"So now," said Ms. Proger, "I must get going." She stood up. She took a scarf from her coat pocket and wrapped it around her neck three times. "I'm glad to see you're taking an interest in history," she said. "Ask me questions whenever you want."

Keith could not go all over town asking about black

dust. It was bad enough to have asked his father and his teacher, each of whom might somehow find out that the other had been asked and start to wonder why. The obvious thing would be to go to the library. But the librarian knew him well, and she knew the kinds of books he liked: mountain-climbing adventures, space-alien invasions, stories about being lost in the wilderness or sailing uncharted oceans. If he started asking for a book about black dust, she'd be curious, and it would be worse if he asked for a book about coal ("which of course we do not use"). She might mention his question to someone else, who could mention it to another person, and soon the question would be going around: "Why is Keith Arlo asking about 'black dust'?" And the secret could come out, and his chance to fly could be gone.

So he did not go to the library. He was pretty sure it wouldn't have helped, anyhow; he didn't think there were a whole lot of books written about things that happened hundreds of years ago.

(Actually, he was wrong about this. Only a few books written during the Sudden Fall made it through the chaos of that time. But in the years afterward, many people had written about those terrible days, hoping that readers would learn not to make the same mistakes twice. There were nine such books in the Cliff River Library. Keith read none of them. Things might have been different if he had.)

9

Floating

Amity Wing, who lived with her parents on the second floor of the Brightspot Apartments, had five best friends: Lottie, Celia, Oates, Neva, and Mandolyn. All of them were twelve years old, all of them high-energy girls with powerful imaginations. After school, on the first Tuesday of the month, they always had a special outing. They did not spend this time studying or being helpful. There was enough of that on all the rest of the days. On first Tuesdays, they did things they invented for themselves.

They had various territories: the boat docks by the river, the back alleys behind the shops, the water towers, the stubs of concrete where the old highway used to be. But lately their favorite place was a pond in the woods at the north of the city. It was a large pond; maybe it was really a small lake, but Amity liked the word "pond," so they called it the pond.

Today they planned to do Floating. Celia was the one carrying their green bag, which held all the things they would need. For this time, there were towels, combs, and a blanket. They had their swim slips on under their clothes. Amity met Celia and Lottie and Neva on the river path, and farther along, by the bakery, Mandolyn and Oates joined up with them, and they all walked along together.

Amity felt the high spirit that goes with having done what you're supposed to do and now being free to do what you want. She breathed in the cool air from the river, and in a way that was almost singing, she said, "If only, if only."

"If only we had a dog with us," Lottie said, striding along.

"If only we had wings and could fly," said Celia, swinging the green bag.

"If only the pond weren't so cold," said Oates.

"No, no!" cried Amity. "You can't say what you *don't* like, you have to say what you *would* like." That was the rule of the game.

"If only," said Oates, "the pond were nice and warm."

"If only a huge, beautiful ship would come up the river," said Neva, "and there would be a black-haired handsome captain who would invite us all on board and we would sail away to some foreign place like Spain or Japan."

"Ha!" said Mandolyn. "If only wishes came true."

They went up the five stone steps at the end of Water Street, they passed the gates of the White Horse Courtyard and the Yarrow Courtyard on 63rd Circle, and after the pavement ended, they went as far as the oak stump, and then turned left along the path through the field of dry grass and followed it until they came to the edge of the forest.

For ten minutes or so, they walked in the shade of the trees, and then they came out into the meadow, where at this season, the last of the small blue wildflowers bloomed in the grass. At the end of the meadow was the pond. Its water was murky and still. On its south bank were some groups of big, rounded rocks that were good for leaning against and for putting things on. This was where the girls settled.

The grass of the meadow was deep yellow. They laid out the cloth for sitting on. Amity went to the edge of the water and put her toe in. "Not too cold," she said. "I'll go in first. We don't have to just float. We can swim or float or dive, whatever we want." She took off her clothes until only her swimming slip—a blue one—was left, and she waded in.

The water was warm at first. Mud and weeds rose around her feet. She kept going until the water was up to her waist, and then she tipped forward and was all in. It was cool, not cold. She swam a few strokes and then turned over and floated on her back. "It's nice!" she called to the others. When she went to stand up, she found that her feet wouldn't touch the bottom, so she paddled a little toward the shore, where Mandolyn stood, ready to come in, and the rest in a bunch behind her.

For a while, all of them paddled around. They splashed each other and laughed. Oates stayed closest to the shore.

"Are there fish in here?" Celia said, waving her legs underwater.

"I feel one, I feel one!" cried Neva.

"Look, here's one!" Mandolyn pulled a stringy wet weed from the water and threw it at Celia, and Celia shrieked and caught it and threw it back.

Amity swam out to the middle of the pond, floated there for a minute, and then called to the others: "I'm diving down!"

She ducked her head under, and the rest of them saw her feet stick up and disappear. Some seconds went by, and then some more. "Where—" said Celia just as Amity's head popped up, her dark hair streaming.

"Something's under there!" she called out. She swam in toward the shore as the others called out questions:

"What is it?"

"Did you touch it?"

"Is it something alive?"

Oates asked nothing—she was too busy scrambling out of the water.

When they were all out, and dried off, and back into

their clothes, they sat on the ground with their feast and talked about it.

"I couldn't see clearly at all under there," Amity said. "But I'm pretty sure it was *something* and not just a rock."

"Did it move?"

"I couldn't tell. Weeds moved around it."

"Were you afraid of it?"

"A little."

"Maybe it was a skeleton!"

"No, it was bigger than that," said Amity.

"I'm never coming to this pond again!" said Oates. "What if it crawled out?"

"I don't think it will," said Amity. "Someday, I'll dive down and look at it up close. All of us can. We'll figure it out."

They finished their feast, which included berry tarts this time, and they packed up and went back into the city. When they got to the Brightspot Apartments, Amity climbed the stairs to the second floor and waved to them all from her bedroom window, as she always did. They waved back. Down the street, Amity saw Keith, who lived upstairs, coming toward home. He saw the girls waving, looked up, saw Amity, and he waved at her, too. She waved back.

10

Gloria

Lulu was getting used to her new life. It wasn't completely different—she lived in the same building, she went to the same school. It was only that her parents weren't there, and her sorrow about that was like a hole in her heart. No, it was more than a hole because of what she knew and couldn't tell. It was like a dark little creature in her heart, biting at her and causing pain.

Still, a lot of the time, she was okay. The Arlo family did their best to make her feel that she belonged. Aunt Meg did, especially. Her injured foot was almost healed, she no longer needed her crutches, and she had finished her doorway design for Power Station 5. So now and then, on an afternoon when Lulu was home from school, she'd say, "How about a little jaunt today?" and the two of them would go out together.

They walked to the Frog Fountain on 27th Street, where you could wade on warm days, and to the Bee Gardens, where you could watch the bees sipping from the flowers, and you could buy honey if you wanted. They went to the Museum of New Colors, full of paintings in which artists tried to use colors no one had seen before. (A few almost succeeded.) They rode their bikes to the River Overlook at the edge of the city, where they tossed twigs into the fast water below and watched them get carried away, and they rode to the end of Cardinal Street to see the famous Deep Steps, which led far down into the ground and then stopped at a wall of rock.

"These are left from the time before," Aunt Meg said, "when people went down into underground tunnels."

"Why?" Lulu asked, but Aunt Meg didn't know.

Lulu loved the jaunts, but fall was turning into winter now, and often the days were cold and rainy. Also, Aunt Meg got another project: to design the balcony railings for a new concert hall.

"I have a splendid idea for them," she told Lulu. "They will be made of iron but look like morning glory vines!"

This meant no more jaunts for a while, but Aunt Meg suggested other things Lulu could do in the hours after school: she could read, or she could play with her new building blocks, or she could go downstairs and help Gloria Garden get organized.

"If I helped Gloria, what would I do?" Lulu asked.

"Gloria's getting older," said Aunt Meg. "The last time I was in her apartment, there was clutter all over. It's hard for her to move around and put things away. You could help her a bit, if you'd like to. I've told her you might come."

That was what Lulu chose to do. After lunch, she went down to the first floor and knocked on Gloria's door. She heard some thumps and grunts, and then the door opened and there was Gloria, with her gap-toothed smile that grew wider and happier when she saw Lulu. "Oh, you came, I am so glad, you're a darling!" said Gloria. She reached out and caught at Lulu's sleeve. "Come in. You'll be a great help, you can see I need it, maybe. A few extra things lying around here and there."

Lulu stepped inside. More than a few things were lying around, though it was hard to see exactly what. There was a sofa over by the windows, draped with several large woolly sweaters, or maybe blankets, along with a lot of pillows. There was a table, completely covered by stacks of papers, piles of cups and plates, many candle stubs, a large basket full of crumpled cloth, and various bags, boxes, and bottles. It was the same all over the room: a jumble of stuff everywhere, so much there was hardly room to walk around.

Gloria plopped herself down on the couch, and a puff of dust flew up. "Have a seat," she said, patting the cushion next to her. "I know what's happened to you, such a sad thing, but now you'll be all right, won't you? But of course always remember."

"Yes," Lulu said, but Gloria just took a breath and went on talking.

"You can see," she said, sweeping a hand across the room, "that I've fallen behind a little, not much, it has to do with getting older, which I am doing!" She laughed and tucked a stray hair behind her ear. "So I'm completely delighted that you can help, a young person's face is so refreshing, I know you're a good, helpful girl. Where shall we start?"

Lulu looked around. "Not to be rude," she said, "but your living room is really messy."

"It is!" cried Gloria. "So we'll start here, I think it's a good idea, we'll do it together."

"And are the other rooms sort of messy, too?" asked Lulu. There was a closed door at the back of the living room.

"Oh, they're all right for now, we won't worry about them."

"I can go check them so we can make a plan." Lulu stood up and started for the door.

"No," said Gloria quite sharply. "Don't go in there. That room is fine. Let's start here."

"I know what," Lulu said. "I'll pick things up one at a time, and you tell me where they go."

"Splendid, dear," Gloria said. "I see you're an organized little person, aren't you? You say what you're going to do and then you do it, I admire that."

Lulu moved around the room. She picked up a dirty sock with a hole in it, a bowl that had broken in half, and a cushion with its stuffing coming out. "What about these? Should we throw them out?"

"Not that bowl," Gloria said. "All it needs is a bit of glue, and that cushion, I know it's coming apart, but it's a favorite of mine. I'll just stitch it up, it will be all right."

Lulu put all these things back where they'd been. She held up the sock. "What about this?"

"I guess I don't need that. I can't find the one it goes with."

Lulu discovered as she went through the chests and cabinets and drawers that Gloria had some beautiful things as well as so many junky things. Often the beautiful things were pushed to the back of a drawer or on a high shelf in a closet and probably hadn't been looked at for a long time. That day she found two beautiful things: a seashell, spotted pink and red, and a silver cup with "Glory" inscribed on it.

Lulu brought these things out and set them down beside Gloria.

"Oh, heavens," said Gloria. "I remember! That cup was from my mother, and that shell—must have picked it up in a shop, I've never been to the seashore, I pick things up all over the place, you know. I've always been a collector."

"The problem is," Lulu said, "you have too much stuff. You can't see the nice things because of the crummy things. That's why you need to get rid of some."

"You don't understand, dear. I need all of these things."

"You don't," said Lulu.

"I *do!*"

Lulu felt very sure about this. "They taught us in school," she said. "It's a rhyme: 'Greed . . . is more than you need.'"

Gloria shook her head and looked away. "No, no. All these things are useful to me or *could* be useful someday."

Lulu was exasperated. "Okay, I know what," she said. "I can just take all these things and put them in another room. That way at least *this* room will be neat."

"Good idea," said Gloria, "we'll do that sometime, but not now, I'm very tired, so we'll stop for today."

"But we haven't done anything! Can't I just peek in the other room to see how much space there is?"

Gloria heaved herself to her feet, grunting and wheezing. "Such good work you've done! But the other room, no. Not now. I'll need to do a little . . . Some other time. But look!" She pointed to a picture hanging on the wall: a brownish boat on a greenish lake. "That painting is hanging crooked! You could fix it, that would be so helpful, and then we'll say goodbye."

Lulu straightened the picture. "Goodbye," she said, and that was all they got done that day.

11

Uninhabitable

The next day, Lulu went down again to help Gloria. She knocked on the door, but no one came. So she tried the door, found it unlocked, and went in.

Gloria was asleep on the sofa, lying on her side. One hand was curled into a fist below her chin, and the other dangled toward the floor. She was snoring loudly. Lulu took her shoes off so she'd make no sound, and she crept across the room toward the closed door. Holding her breath, she turned the knob.

But there was no room. What she saw was a jumbly wall of bags and crates and boxes and suitcases, stacked one on top of the other and blocking the doorway all the way to the ceiling. A smell drifted out, not a good one, and she heard a tiny skittering noise. She couldn't hold back a small shriek of surprise. She closed the door, but the shriek woke Gloria.

"Who's there?" she cried, hoisting herself up.

"Just me," Lulu said.

Gloria slumped against the pillows. "I told you we can't use that room. That room is full."

"We could clear it out," said Lulu, but she said it weakly. She knew she wasn't strong enough for that job. Anyhow, she didn't want to do it. All that stinky junk crammed in there—it scared her.

"Some other day," said Gloria, lying back down.

Lulu went out the front door and up the stairs. At home, she told her aunt Meg about Gloria's apartment.

"A whole *room* full of stuff?" Aunt Meg said. "And a *smell*? I had no idea. Come with me." She led Lulu downstairs. On the way she said, "It's okay to have a lot of stuff, as long as it doesn't get in the way of other people's lives."

"But what if it only gets in the way of *her* life?" Lulu asked.

"She can live like that if she wants to. But she'll soon have rats and bugs and even fires, if she doesn't already. Those would get in everyone's way."

When Gloria opened the door, Aunt Meg stepped into the room without waiting to be invited. She went to the bedroom door and looked at the wall of stuff. Then she came back and said firmly and kindly, "Gloria, you have too many things. You have more than you can keep track of, more than you can keep clean, way more than you need. Whole families of mice and rats could be hiding in here, and you wouldn't even know. We'd like to help you clear out a bit."

"No," said Gloria. "I like my house the way it is, I know where everything is, and all of it is important and useful."

"We'll see," said Aunt Meg. As she and Lulu went up the stairs, she said, "We're going to need help. I'll organize it."

The next day, after breakfast, Aunt Meg said, "Lulu, how about if you take Gloria out for a shopping trip? Today there's a street market a couple of blocks away. Gloria would love it. Stay away for at least two or three hours."

While Lulu and Gloria were shopping, eleven people—Keith, his parents, and all the members of his soccer team, plus Amity Wing and her parents—were moving Gloria's belongings out of the house and onto four large donkey carts parked outside. Aunt Meg supervised. "Empty out the bedroom and the living room," she told them. "Get rid of everything except what Gloria needs and some nice extras."

Keith was horrified by Gloria's apartment. She had stuffed it so full that she could barely live in it. "Uninhabitable" was the word that came to him. It was what happened when your trash got bigger than the place where you lived.

Amity, like Keith, found the apartment awful—not just

95

because it was uninhabitable, but because it was so far from beautiful. Amity wanted everything to be beautiful—herself, her home, her city—and when she encountered ugliness, she always had a strong urge to fix it. Gloria's apartment gave her a sinking feeling because it looked almost unfixable. But she pitched in, lifting boxes and bags, holding her breath against the smell.

She was the one who saw the rat. She was not a screaming type of girl, but she couldn't help a quick scream when the furry gray creature ran across her foot. She managed to trap it under a bucket, and Frank, one of Keith's friends, slid a scrap of cardboard underneath and took the rat away.

It proved impossible to get everything out of Gloria's house in the time they had; but still, the rooms looked airy and only somewhat cluttered by the time Gloria and Lulu got back from shopping.

Then came the hard part.

Gloria came in, chatting away. "We had the best time, didn't we, Lulu? The market was full of wonderful—" She stopped and looked around. "Where is everything?"

Aunt Meg came up behind her. "Isn't it lovely, Gloria? So neat and spacious? We did a little cleaning up while you were gone."

Gloria exploded. She yelled, she wailed, she called them all thieves and vandals and criminals, and over and over, she said, "Those things were *mine*! I needed *all* of them!"

"We know it's kind of a shock, Gloria," said Aunt Meg.

"But it had to be done. We found three rats' nests in your bedroom, two of them with babies in them. You can start collecting again right away, if you want to."

They left Gloria shouting and wailing.

"We'll need to keep an eye on Gloria," Aunt Meg said as they went up the stairs. "She mustn't get her house in that state again."

"How will we do that?" Lulu asked. "I'm sure she's so mad at us she won't let us in."

"True. We'll have to think about it."

"Were the rat babies cute?" Lulu asked.

"No," said Aunt Meg. "They were squirmy little pink blobs."

"What did you do with them?"

"They have been relocated."

Lulu imagined the rat families making nests in the leaves, out in the forest.

12

Trouble with Secrets

As Keith went down the stairs one bright, cold afternoon, heading out to his ball game, he saw the mailman coming toward him. "Hey, Keith Arlo," said the mailman. "I have a letter addressed to you." He rummaged around in his pack and handed over a light blue envelope. There was no return address, but the handwriting looked familiar—squarish, sticklike letters. It took him a few seconds—he hadn't seen that writing for more than three months—but then he remembered.

He folded the letter and put it in his pocket. He would save it until after the game. All afternoon, as he ran with Hale and Anders and Pelo and Frank on the East Field, he could feel it there, almost as if it were a live thing, whispering to him, telling him to hurry up and read it. He was so distracted that he made a few mistakes, kicking the ball the wrong direction. Frank said, "What's wrong with you? You never do that."

"I just missed it, that's all."

"You're kind of far away lately. Is something going on?"

Keith wanted to say, *Yes! I flew! And now I've got a letter from Malcolm!* Instead he said, "A few things." That, of course, made his friends curious. They pestered Keith to tell them more, and Keith wished he'd said nothing.

When the game was over at last, he raced home and went straight to his room, where he took the letter from his pocket and sat on the window ledge and opened the envelope. Inside were two pages of light blue paper, printed with the square writing he knew was Malcolm's. He read:

Greetings, Keith!

I have some news for you. We are getting closer to our Grand Introduction, which will take place in your city. I have been talking with the team about an exciting idea. What would you say to appearing in our show?

Your role would be simple: you would fly, as you did before. The thousands watching will be astounded. They will want to fly, too. You will be their inspiration!

What do you think? I feel sure you'll

want to grab this opportunity. We'll
need to meet beforehand, to talk about
how it's all going to work and do a bit
more practice. You'd need to come again
to Graves Mountain. Eleven o'clock on
Wednesday the 12th-can you do that?
   Reply to this letter as soon as possible.
                    Malcolm Quinsmith,
                       Project F Director

Yes, Keith said to himself. Yes, I want to do it.

The problem was that he would miss a day of school. He would need a reason not to be there.

"Lulu," he said later, after dinner. It was a good moment to talk, because his mother was working on her morning glory design, and his father had gone downstairs to take an evening walk by the river. "I want to ask you something," Keith said.

"Okay." Lulu was sitting at the dinner table with the small battery lamp beside her. She was doing her school assignment, which was to draw three kinds of extinct animals, copying from pictures the teacher had given them. The light made a bright circle on the paper. With a blue pencil, she started on the whale.

"You know how I flew that day?" Keith said. "You remember?"

"Sure."

"What did you think, when you saw me do that?"

Lulu looked up at him with a slight frown. She had her hair in one braid down her back today instead of two pigtails, and it was tied with a yellow piece of yarn. She was taller. She would be seven, he remembered, in another month.

"It was great, sort of," she said.

"Just sort of? Why?"

"I don't know. It's a little bit ugly."

"Ugly?!"

"I don't mean *you*. I mean the noise, and the smell. When a real bird flies, it's more beautiful." She moved her arms up and down like wings.

"Of course," Keith said. "A bird is made for flying."

"And we aren't."

"But just because we aren't made for it doesn't mean we shouldn't do it."

"*I* don't know," Lulu said. She went back to her work, finishing the blue whale. "Why are you asking me all this?"

"Because I want you to remember how important it is," said Keith. "I have to go and see Malcolm again, which means missing school, and I have to keep it a secret. So on Wednesday, would you tell my teachers that I won't be there because I'm not feeling good?"

"Okay. But it's not true."

"No. But it's very important for me to go. You can probably guess why."

"You're going to fly again."

"Right. And pretty soon, everybody will know about it—so no more secrets to keep."

"Good," Lulu said in a grumpy way. "I have too many secrets already."

Keith was surprised at this. Too many? He'd thought she had just the one. But he didn't ask about it; he didn't want to make her even grumpier.

She went back to her drawing. She was drawing an elephant now. For the third one, she would have to choose between a panda and a gorilla.

"Remember—Wednesday," Keith said. "That's a week from tomorrow. Can you promise me you'll do it?"

"Yes, yes, I will." Lulu put a tail on the elephant—such a huge, wonderful animal!—and started working on the gorilla. It had a wrinkled face and kind eyes. "Why did some animals go extinct?" she asked.

"I'm not sure," Keith said. "Not enough food?"

"I don't think that's right." Lulu decided to draw the panda, too, even though that would be four instead of three. The panda was extremely cute.

Once she'd finished drawing, Lulu sat doing nothing for a while, having uneasy thoughts. She felt she was doing a wrong thing by telling lies, but it would also be a wrong thing to give away Keith's secret. She felt stuck. She decided to go downstairs and visit Amity. It was something she used to do now and then, and she hadn't done it since she'd begun living with her new family. She told Aunt Meg where she was going, and she went down the two flights of stairs and knocked on the Wings' door.

Mrs. Wing answered. She was a short, slim person with black hair in a plain, straight cut. Today she was wearing blue pants and a tunic of lighter blue. She smiled at Lulu. "You're looking for Amity, I suppose. Please come in."

Lulu knew that Amity's mother sometimes worked as a chef in a downtown restaurant, and that her father was a fisherman on a riverboat. Their house was very different from the Arlos' house, even though the plan of the rooms was the same. Here, the rooms felt airy, even when the windows weren't open. Leafy plants in pots stood by the windows. The chairs had wood frames and light green cushions. All the drawings on the walls were of river scenes or of fish in pale, shimmering colors. Right now, there was a scent of lemon in the air, maybe from tea.

Lulu found Amity in her room. She was turned away, looking out the window. Her dark hair fell down her back almost to her waist. Lulu said, "Knock, knock! I've come to see you."

"Lulu!" said Amity. "Come over here."

Lulu stood beside her.

"See that?" Amity pointed out the window, but Lulu saw only ordinary things: someone many blocks away hanging

laundry on a line, a boat going slowly by on the river, someone running on the river path. "See what?" said Lulu.

"Those clothes on the line! The colors are gorgeous!"

Lulu saw that it was true. The clothes flapping in the
breeze—too far away to know if they were shirts or skirts
or what—were orange like flames, and bright red, and
sunny yellow, and some deep plum color that was either
blue or purple. She wouldn't have noticed, but Amity could
always pick out what was beautiful.

"Now you do it," Amity said. "Find a beautiful thing
out there."

Lulu pointed down to the street. "The blanket on
that donkey," she said, "striped white and green. Is that
beautiful?"

"Absolutely." Amity sat down on the window seat, facing Lulu. "How are you?" she said.

"All right. Most of the time. Sometimes."

"And sometimes not?"

"Yes."

"Right now, not so great?"

Lulu nodded. She knew that Amity thought she was
sad because of her parents, and that was true, she was. But
there was something else about what had happened on the
seashore that she didn't know, another secret Lulu was
keeping. And of course Amity didn't know about Keith
flying and all the lies she'd told. Should she tell her about
these things? Would that make the bad feelings better?

105

She said, "I have some secrets—" but then her throat seemed to close up.

"What secrets?" Amity asked.

Lulu couldn't speak because her throat was so tight.

"It would be all right to tell me," Amity said.

But Lulu shook her head. The words wouldn't come.

"Never mind," Amity said. "Would you like me to do your hair in a bun?"

Lulu said she would, and when, after half an hour, Amity had finished brushing her hair and sweeping it upward and fastening it into a sort of doughnut on her head, and Lulu saw herself in the mirror, she thought she looked very wise and calm, and quite a bit older, maybe eight.

13

The Three Tests

Keith left early on the Wednesday of his trip. It was chilly; high clouds blocked the sun. He caught the train as before and found a seat easily, since there were only a few passengers. On his first trip, he had felt the excitement of a new adventure; this time his excitement was just as high, but it was accompanied by a thrilling sort of darkness. His mission was secret. No one (except Lulu) knew where he was. And he'd be doing something few people in the world had ever done. He had on his canvas hat, and he pulled its brim down over his forehead, like a spy who doesn't want to be seen. He'd brought along his book about space aliens, but it seemed trivial to him now. Anyway, he was too excited to read it.

He was in no danger of falling asleep, as Malcolm had before. The world outside the train windows always interested him, even though the gray sky made everything look dim and flat. The fields were empty now, just big spaces of dark earth, and wagons stood empty next to them, except for some loaded with wood, heading back toward the city. No bikers rode the path by the train.

At the first stop—the tiny town where Malcolm had got on—a few more passengers boarded, including a man carrying a loaf of just-baked bread, which gave the train car a wonderful smell. "Lovely!" exclaimed a woman sitting behind Keith as the man passed, and he smiled at her and pulled a chunk off the loaf and gave it to her. Seeing that Keith was watching, he gave him a bit, too. Keith said "Thanks!" and the man said "Quite welcome!" and passed into the next car. Something about riding on a train, Keith thought—it could make people feel warm and connected and generous.

After that, it was woods and woods, curves right and left, and no stops at all until Graves Mountain, where the shabby little station looked exactly the same, even with the same crumpled peanut packets on the floor. No one was there, so Keith started up the road among the trees, and in a few minutes, he saw Malcolm striding toward him. He was wearing a long jacket that flapped in the wind, and around his neck a scarf striped turquoise and maroon.

"There you are!" he cried, raising a hand. "Right on time." When he came near, he clapped Keith on the shoulder and turned to walk with him. Keith had to speed up.

"I knew you'd grab this chance," Malcolm said. "I could see it in your eyes last time—the spirit of adventure."

"That's right. How could I resist?"

"Of course you couldn't."

A gust of wind moved through the tree branches. Keith held his hat on.

They reached the gate and went through onto the field, and then across to the buildings. It was lunchtime by then, and once again, the room was filled with people and good food smells. They ate, and Malcolm talked. He looked scruffier, Keith thought. His shirt was grimy around the neck, his hair had grown shaggy, and his middle looked a bit pudgier than before.

"We've put a few new features on the Model F," Malcolm said. "It has more boost. And we've made the fuel tank slightly bigger, which means you can go farther. Really, the thing is just spectacular."

"And have you flown it yourself?" Keith asked.

"Not yet," Malcolm said. "We're still working on the larger size. The Model F.2 will be the one for me." He swiped his hand across his mouth, making a slight soup stain at one corner, and stood up. He gave a signal to one of his men, and he and Keith went out onto the field, the men coming behind with the equipment.

"I'd like to put you through three tests," Malcolm said. "Are you willing?"

"Of course." It was early afternoon by now. The sun

was high in the sky, but it was only a smudge of light behind the clouds. Trees stood all the way around the field like silent people, watching.

"The three tests are these," Malcolm said. "How fast can you fly? How high can you go? And how far can you go?"

"All right," Keith said. He felt ready for anything.

"Load him up," Malcolm told the men, and they strapped and buckled the Model F onto him. It felt slightly heavier than before.

"First, how fast. It doesn't matter where you go," Malcolm said. He had a clipboard with him, and a pencil. "Just back and forth across the field will be fine. Check the speedometer as often as you can. Keep turning the dial for more and more power, until you can feel that you're right on the edge of losing control. How fast are you going at that moment? Remember the number."

The wind dropped. Everything was still.

"Ready?"

"Ready," answered Keith. Only that one word was in his mind. He felt like an arrow.

He grasped the control bars. Dodge bent behind him, and he heard the scratch of the match and felt the heat of the rockets.

"Go!" cried Malcolm right in his ear, and he flipped the switch and felt the earth falling away beneath him. He rose above the trees and then leveled out and began turning up his speed. Back and forth over the field, a little faster each time, his hair whipping at his face, the ground a blur below him—until he felt a sort of wobble and heard a high unnatural shriek from the engines. The number on the dial was 58. He cut back the speed and came down, landing with a thump and a stagger.

"Fifty-eight," he said when he'd come to a stop.

"Excellent!" said Malcolm, and the guys on the team applauded a little. "Could you have gone any faster, do you think?"

Keith told about the wobble and the shriek.

"Okay, good. We don't want the machine to fly apart, do we?"

No, Keith thought. Or me, either.

They went on from there to the next test: How High.

For this one, Keith started climbing right after takeoff. He went as steeply as he could. A small dial on the dashboard told him how many feet up he'd gone, but he kept forgetting to look at it. His eyes were on the clouds that lay like a ceiling overhead. Would he shoot through them? Bump into them? He was high, high above the ground now; the buildings were like a child's blocks, Malcolm and Dodge were like bugs. But long before he reached the clouds, he felt the wobble and heard the shriek, and he cut his speed and went down.

"Seven hundred and fourteen," he told the team. They were pleased.

"We'll refuel and try it a couple more times," Malcolm said.

Dodge, carrying a metal cylinder, stood behind Keith and did something to the backpack—unsnapped a chamber, it sounded like. Then there was a *tap-tap* sound as he poured in the contents of the cylinder. Keith couldn't see any of this, naturally; he would have had to turn his head all the way around, like an owl.

He did the height test three more times, each time forcing himself just a little farther past the wobble and shriek. His final number was 810. Malcolm seemed content with that.

"Now How Far," Malcolm said. "This one is trickier. See that ridge over there?" He pointed to the hills that rose behind the buildings. "I want you to go over that ridge until you see a range of strange-looking hills beyond it. Your goal is to fly far enough so that you can tell me what those hills are made of when you get back."

"What if there's the wobble and shriek before I get there?"

"Then, as before, you'll have to turn around. I don't think that will happen, though. Just take a straight route. It isn't far."

So, after another refueling, Keith rose again, flew over the buildings, and crossed over the ridge. The rockets buzzed steadily, warming his back and legs. Right away, he saw the low hills. They were more like heaps or mounds

than hills. They were an odd reddish color, and their surface was lumpy and jagged. Grass and weeds grew on them,
and here and there a twisted, scrawny tree. The line of hills
went on and on, winding to the north for what looked like
miles. In the distance, something very thin and tall stood
beside the hills, in the shape of an upside-down V, like a
monster with its neck broken.

Keith circled around and around, going slowly, getting
as close as he could, trying to spot something that would
give him the answer to Malcolm's question. What were
these odd hills made of? He saw a glint in the land below,
as if maybe the hills were made of glass. Or maybe metal,
catching a beam of light when the sun emerged now and
then from the darkening clouds. He turned his speed down
as low as he dared, until he was skimming no more than
twenty feet above the hilltops, and he peered down. Ir-
regular shapes, just below the ground. But what were they?

He knew the Model F's wobble and shriek would come
soon. No more exploring—he would have to go back. He
upped his speed and turned around.

He landed perfectly, without a single extra step.

"And what are those hills made of?" Malcolm asked
him.

"I don't know," Keith said. "I got close to them, but
I still couldn't tell. Something in them sparkles. Maybe
metal?"

"Absolutely," Malcolm said. His voice rose, and he

was suddenly angry. "Those hills are the ruined remains of the central glory of the most brilliant civilization that ever existed! They represent a terrible crime—a vast destruction—a horrible mistake."

It was alarming, how furious Malcolm had become, just in a moment. He was shaking. His face was red. Dodge had a solemn look and was nodding slightly, as if he knew just what Malcolm was upset about and completely agreed.

"I don't understand," Keith said.

Malcolm took a long breath. "What you saw," he said, "is Demo Depot #17 East, more commonly known as Range 17 of the Car Mountains. All over the country, there are ancient graveyards like this one, made up of the millions of cars and trucks and motorcycles that were outlawed, hauled off, crushed, and piled up during the Sudden Fall. There are Airline Mountains, too, full of planes and helicopters. Miracles of engineering! The key to a life of freedom! Now home to rats. Dead, rusting, used for scavenging. You might have noted the crane out there, still trying to pull usable materials out of the heap. In the past, there was tons of it. The metal you see in your buildings, your trains, your bikes, your fences—that's where it came from!" He thrust out his arm, pointing a furious finger toward the Car Mountains.

"And so the Model F . . . ," Keith said uncertainly.

"Gets us on the road again," Malcolm said. "So to speak. Gets us *above* the road. Moving forward and up."

"And the reason the cars were destroyed was . . . ?" Keith waited, but Malcolm was writing on his clipboard and not paying attention.

Keith tried again. "Why *were* the cars turned into junk? If they were wonderful?"

Malcolm glanced at him, frowning. "A problem of heat," he said. "According to some, at least. Others disagreed."

"So you mean the cars were causing that? Why didn't they just fix the cars?"

Malcolm said, without looking up from his notes, "Had a book about all that once—seem to have mislaid it. Doesn't matter—terrible book." He put the notes aside and gave Keith a faint, distracted smile. "We will be in touch soon about the Introduction."

"Great," said Keith. He of course knew the "terrible book" Malcolm had mislaid, since he had it himself. Time to take a closer look at it, maybe.

The train ride home seemed very long. It rained the whole way, so darkness came early, and there was nothing to see out the window but his own reflection. Something troubled him about what he'd seen at Graves Mountain, and he was troubled as well by Malcolm's suddenly violent outburst, and by the way he avoided answering certain questions. Probably, though, this didn't mean there was anything wrong about him. He was passionate about his project, that was all, and he had a lot of important things on his mind.

14

Fashion

It was a first Tuesday again, and Amity and the girls were setting out for the woods.

This time, someone extra was with them. Neva had asked if she could bring her cousin Dellis, who was visiting from Papermill City. "I don't really know her very well," Neva had said, "but she seems okay, and she's bored sitting around with the old people."

Amity had said yes, though she hesitated. She wasn't happy about adding another person. But this cousin would go home soon. One day with her wouldn't matter.

It was chilly. Gray-white clouds skimmed over the sky. The cousin was a chunky girl with an eager smile and a way of talking in a constant stream as she walked. "Do you girls know Missy Bard?" she said. "She lives in your city. I met her once when I went to a music contest.

She plays the flute. I play the drums." All the girls said they didn't know her, but Dellis went on. "Everyone in my family plays an instrument, even my grandfather. He plays the horn. He can't walk very well and can't climb stairs, and that's why we live on the first floor of our house."

They went through the boatyard, where a sailboat loaded with crates was just pulling up to a dock. Nuts from the north might be in those crates, or maybe jars of maple syrup. The girls walked quickly. Dellis had to break into a trot now and then to keep up with them.

"I'm a pretty good walker," said Dellis. "From our house to the city center is eighteen blocks, and I can walk that far in twenty-seven minutes. I timed it. I don't walk so far very often, though, mostly I just walk to school, which is only eight minutes away. I've never been to a forest before."

"If only, if only," sang Amity.

"If only we could find a jewel buried in the ground," Lottie chimed in.

"If only the flock of black geese would come today," said Mandolyn.

"If only I'd remembered to bring my sweater," said Oates, shivering.

"If only we could ride through the woods on horseback and find a castle," said Neva.

Amity said, "Now you, Dellis."

"Okay. If only I had on a red shirt instead of this old

brown one I'm wearing, because red looks better on me, and this brown one is missing a button and it doesn't fit me very well. I actually do have a red shirt, but it was in the wash today, otherwise I would have worn it."

They passed the stump, turned, crossed the field, and came to the pond. Its water looked dark gray. They settled down near the big rocks.

Today they were going to do Fashions.

Celia spread out the contents of the green bag—shirts, scarves, dresses, nightgowns, stockings. She draped them over the rocks and on the grassy patches on the ground. For the last few weeks, the girls had been collecting these things, all of them castoffs because they were torn or stained or just limp from long wear.

Amity explained to Dellis. "What we do is take these old ratty things and make them into beautiful things."

"I'm not sure how to do that," said Dellis. "I never learned sewing because I don't have the right kind of skill with my fingers. My fingers are better for drums and building things and—"

"It doesn't matter," Amity said. "You can just put things together however you want. We use a lot of pins."

Neva took two pairs of scissors and a box of pins from her pack, and Amity brought out two balls of yarn, one black and one yellow. Mandolyn had miscellaneous—ribbons, feathers, beads, belts, bracelets. And Lottie had the feast, which they would eat later.

They set to work, cutting, pinning, tying knots, and talking and talking.

"Tie some of this pink nightie to the black stockings."

"No, that looks terrible!"

"Give me the scissors, I'm going to make a scarf with beads on it."

"Beautiful!"

"But not done yet! Cut that part into a fringe!"

Amity loved beautiful things. The old clothes were not beautiful, but when you cut them up and put them together in new ways, they could become beautiful. Or at least wild and strange. She liked to make herself beautiful, too. Her hair was long and dark, and she changed its style all the time—braided it and twisted it and piled it up on her head and fastened it with yarn. Her clothes were plain, white or gray or cream-colored, but she always added one bright thing. Today it was her red shoes. In her chest of drawers at home, she had a green woven belt, and a necklace of blue stones, and fourteen scarves, all different.

Dellis was struggling. She had tied together a white dish towel, some gray-striped rags, and a flowered bandanna. Her idea was to make a shirt. But she wasn't pleased with it. She couldn't get it to look pretty.

"Try weaving in this purple stocking," said Neva.

"Or some ribbons by the neck," said Mandolyn.

Dellis tried, making grumpy sounds as she worked.

When everyone was ready, they did their fashion show,

making the long scarves and capes and flags twirl in the breeze. All except Dellis, who said she wouldn't be in the show because her fashion hadn't turned out right. "I made it too big in the shoulders," she said, "and it doesn't really have sleeves. If there had been more pretty material I could have done it better, and if I'd had more time."

They ate their feast when the sun was just over the tallest pine. Some wasps came to investigate the pumpkin tarts, and Oates shrieked and flung her tart away half-eaten. Now the wasps had her tart and she had nothing.

Suddenly, Dellis jumped up. "Look!" she cried. She pointed to an orange-and-black butterfly hovering over a weed blossom. With a quick swoop, she caught the butterfly in her fist, and with the other hand she snatched up a pin. She flattened the butterfly on the blanket and drove the pin through its body. All this took only a few seconds. The girls were speechless, mouths dropped open.

The butterfly's wings stopped moving. "Now," said Dellis, "I'll have something pretty for my shirt. I'll just stick it on there with the pin."

"No!" cried Amity. "That was a wrong, wrong thing to do!"

And the others chimed in. "How could you do that?"

"Don't you know about being in the woods? Harm nothing! Leave everything as you found it!"

"Leave the animals alone!"

Dellis looked stunned. "It's just a bug," she said.

Neva spoke up for her cousin. "She's never been in the woods before. She doesn't understand."

But the fun of the day was ruined. The breeze blew a little colder, the pond water rippled, and behind the range of hills to the north, lead-gray clouds rose.

They packed everything and hiked back along the path. Amity thought about the butterfly. Yes, it was a bug. There were thousands like it. But the way Dellis killed it without a thought, just for herself—that was the wrong. She had killed it as if it were nothing, as if it were a scrap of trash. Doing it hadn't hurt her heart at all. Amity hadn't known many people like that before.

They went home the way they had come, and when they got to 63rd Street, the rain began to fall. They all ran. Amity was soaked by the time she got to the Brightspot Apartments, but she didn't mind. She ran up to the second floor, scattering drops around her, and from her room she looked out the window to the street, where Neva and Celia and Mandolyn and Oates and Lottie were standing, windblown and wet, looking up. Dellis was talking, but luckily, Amity couldn't hear her over the sound of the rain. She waved at her friends, and they waved at her, as they always did after one of these excursions, and then they went on their way. A block away, Amity saw Keith heading for home, so she waited a minute until he was close enough to see her, and they waved to each other.

15

Keith Reads the Book

A few days later, Keith's parents and Lulu put the family laundry in sacks and baskets and went to the Washington down the street, where many people gathered on Sundays. Keith's mother loved laundry day—she dumped the laundry in the tub and then played her flute with whatever other musicians were there. Lulu always found a couple of friends to talk to and play checkers with.

Keith stayed home. Since the three tests, and Malcolm's sudden anger, he'd wanted to know more about how the world had changed long ago—especially, how all those cars had ended up being dumped. He thought he might find something useful in Malcolm's book. He was going to read it, this time all of it, not just random bits and pieces. He settled on the window seat in the morning sunlight. Down in the street, two donkeys were pulling a red wagon full of crates of potatoes. Keith watched them for a minute, and then he picked up the book.

The first page was blank except for a quotation:

> We have come to the end of the line. We cannot keep living this way unless we wish to destroy our world and ourselves. Now we must act.
>
> **Queen Eleanor**

A queen! But what country was she queen of? Keith had never heard of her.

A great many of the next pages had been ripped out. What was left included the part he had read to Lulu, about when "a treasure was discovered deep in the earth that seemed like magic." Also the part about the "powerful energy" that built the spectacular old world. He skipped over those and began at a chapter called "The First Decree."

> *It has become a famous moment. The king and queen stood side by side, neither one taller than the other, both looking grave and resolute, both still handsome though they were no longer young.*
>
> *The queen spoke first. "For many years, we've talked about what to do—we have held conferences, we have tracked data, we have laid out plans and tried advanced technologies. We have made sincere efforts, but not enough of them. Our*

world grows more and more strange to us. Wild-fires sweep through the land every summer—walls of flame. The sea rises and drowns our cities. Furious storms wreck everything in their path. The ocean warms, and its creatures die. Earth and air are full of poisons. This must not go on. We must act. Today we will issue our First Decree."

"It is very simple," the king said. "We will stop using fossil fuels."

All over the country, the television audience held its breath, waiting for him to explain how we would do this.

"It would have been less painful," the king continued, "if we had started sooner. But we have waited too long. If we go on like this, the world will become uninhabitable—for human beings and animals and thousands of other forms of life. We must live a different way." He paused a moment, and when he spoke, his voice was both stern and sad. "As I said—we will stop using fossil fuels. We will stop tomorrow."

The people in the TV audience turned to each other wide-eyed. Some of them thought the king was joking or using a form of speech in which "tomorrow" stood for "fairly soon." But this was not the case.

The king gave his orders: Tomorrow, he said,

all gas stations would close. Oil and gas storage tanks would be sealed up. The flow of oil and gas through pipelines would stop. Coal mines would close, and so would all electric power plants that burned coal or gas. He went on with this list for quite some time.

The queen took over then: "As we are speaking to you, leaders of all the nations of the world are saying the same to their people. The armies of our nation and all others are ready to help us carry out these orders."

"We will conclude by saying it one more time," said the king. "The way to stop using fossil fuels is to stop using them. We admit that this will cause terrible trouble for the human race; but otherwise, the human race will continue to cause such terrible trouble to the natural world that we will not survive."

What happened then was a vast and deadly global cataclysm.

Keith looked up from the page. He could feel his shoulder muscles tightening, as if the cataclysm were right outside the window. He read on:

How to even begin to talk about something so enormous?

Start with one family. Call them the Hills, John, Helen, and their four children. As soon as they heard the king and queen's announcement, they all jumped in their car and rushed to the supermarket to stock up. Surely they could buy enough food and supplies to keep them going until this nonsense was over. At the market, they found that hundreds of other families had had the same idea. Crowds swarmed through the aisles, jostling and snatching, and it wasn't long before the shelves were empty of useful things (a few plastic toys were left).

The next day, John drove in search of other stores. He drove a long way. Most of the stores he passed had broken windows. When he looked in, he saw wrecked shelves. All the gas stations were closed. Armed guards stood outside them. John began to think the "nonsense" was real. He turned around so that he could make it home before his car ran out of gas, but he didn't turn soon enough. The car slowed and stopped about a mile from his house, and he had to leave it and walk the rest of the way, having bought nothing.

The same thing happened to thousands and thousands of people. Before a month was out, the streets and highways were littered with abandoned cars. People ran out of whatever they had managed to buy. They tapped frantically at their phones, trying to order products to be delivered, but there was a shortage of this and a shortage of that, and anyhow, hardly any vehicles other than bicycles were out there delivering things.

Remember: this was happening all over the world, in all places that depended on fossil fuels, which was nearly everywhere. All the jet planes that flew passengers and cargo all over the world, all the powerful ships that carried millions of products across the oceans, freight trains that hauled loads of grain or fruit or lumber, and almost all the big, heavy trucks that cruised the highways night and day, delivering to stores the things people needed—imagine all of these gone, because all of them ran on fossil fuels. This was what happened, all of a sudden, everywhere.

It was chaos. It only got worse as time went on and people grew more desperate. Sometimes, chaos brought out the best in human nature. Cities put up Help Centers, which distributed things like farm produce and canned food and milk powder, and which treated ill or injured people. Neighbors shared what they had (those who'd been growing vegetable gardens gave out tomatoes and zucchinis). Too often, however, especially as time went on, chaos brought out the worst. There simply

wasn't enough of everything, and those who could
take what they wanted by force did so. Looters rav-
aged stores and houses; battles raged at closed and
guarded gas stations. Armies rose up and fought
against other armies. In many places, electricity
went out, and the chaos hurtled on in the dark.
Even worse—

Many pages were ripped out here, at least six or eight.
Keith tried to imagine what might be even worse than what
he'd just read. Did people starve? Did they kill each other?
Did they go to war and drop bombs? Were there plagues?
What happened to the Hill family?

He turned the page and came to these final paragraphs:

The king and queen and all the other rulers of the
world looked on in anguish. If only, if only, they
said to each other. If only we had found solutions
faster and it had not come to this. If only we had
been willing to say no to those treasures from the
earth, bit by bit, starting a long, long time ago.
They watched as the human world crumbled.

Before the most terrible years were over, they
themselves grew old and died, so they didn't see
how people began, very slowly, over one century
and then another, learning a new way of life amid
the ruins of the old.

In the end, the natural world was saved, and therefore so was the human race, though only a small fraction of it. The planet's climate settled at a temperature in which human beings could live more or less comfortably, at least in certain areas, and live without doing damage to their world. Little by little, they figured things out. They embraced their circumstances and moved forward.

Malcolm had crossed out the word "forward" and printed "backward!!" in dark sticklike letters over it.

At the end of the book were two colored photographs facing each other. The first was a daytime picture of a city, taken from far above. The buildings were unbelievably tall, so tall that the streets looked to be deep down in high-walled pits, full of shiny bits of red, black, white, and yellow—cars and buses, Keith guessed, lined up like beetles. Colored bits swarmed the sidewalks, too—these must be the people, so many they blended into one bright stream. High in the sky above it all was an airplane that looked smaller than a toy, nose tilted upward, maybe ready to cross the ocean.

The second picture showed the same city at night. Bright windows lit the buildings, turning them into enormous checkerboards of black and gold, and down in the streets, the cars had their own lights, white and red. Lit-up signs and images were everywhere, pink, green, yellow, red—brilliant, gorgeous.

Below these pictures, Malcolm had written: "We can have it again!"

Can we? Keith asked himself. Surely we can, if we work hard and do it right. He longed to live in a speedy, sparkling world like that. Malcolm was showing the way.

Still, some questions niggled at him: He knew that oil, coal, and gas were fossil fuels, but what did that mean? The only fossil he had ever seen was a piece of rock with an ancient fish skeleton drawn on it. Surely coal had nothing to do with fish. Had Ms. Proger ever explained this? He couldn't remember.

(In fact, Ms. Proger had given a lesson on this very subject, but because Keith was caught up in an adventure daydream, he didn't listen. If he had, he would have learned that what we call fossil fuels used to be living plants and animals, like the fish preserved on the rock. When they died, millions of years ago, they ended up deeply buried in the earth, where their remains were transformed by time and pressure to rock, in the case of coal, and liquid, in the case of oil. Enormous energy was stored in these remains, which people did not discover and begin to use until just a few centuries ago.)

The most bothersome question for Keith was this: Was "black dust" a fossil fuel? Was it coal dust? He wasn't sure, and he couldn't ask anyone, because if he did, he'd be giving away Malcolm's secret. And if black dust *was* a fossil fuel, then Project F was going to cause harm in some way. But what way? (Again, he would have known if he'd listened that day: years of burning fossil fuels heated up the climate and made the planet a more and more hazardous place for people and other creatures to live in.)

Keith understood that if he knew Project F used fossil fuel, he should have no part in it. He shouldn't fly.

Better not to know.

16

What If . . . ?

Keith started having dreams about flying. In them, he would gather a certain strong feeling within himself, right below his ribs; he would spread his arms and lift off from the ground. It would take some effort, as if he were pushing a column of force down toward the earth, but when he got above the tallest trees, he could swoop and glide like a bird riding currents of air. He woke from these dreams filled with longing. If only, if only he could really fly. He would, soon. It wouldn't be quite the same as in the dreams, but it was the closest he'd ever come.

He also thought about where he'd go once he had his Model F. These were real plans, not dreams. He wanted to fly up the river to the waterfall he knew was to the north. He wanted to fly out over the forest and land in a clearing somewhere—anywhere would be a place he'd never seen before. And, if the new Model F could hold enough fuel, he would go all the way to the ocean and watch the sailing ships come in.

It was almost spring now, not long until the Model F Grand Introduction. Keith was unbearably impatient.

Some afternoons, when he would otherwise have been doing his homework, he worked on an idea that had been growing in his mind. Since the words "black dust" were not mentioned in Malcolm's book, he had decided that black dust must not be a fossil fuel and would therefore not cause damage. So, he reasoned, if black dust was powerful enough to lift a person into the air, why not use it for other things, too? Why not, for instance, use it to propel people on the land? Why not use it to run trains so they could go faster, and why not bring back cars? No doubt Malcolm had thought of these ideas and was planning to work on them once the Model F was up and running.

But in the meantime, Keith could think about them. How would it be to have cars on city streets? They would be quiet, unlike the creaky, rattling wagons. They would keep out the rain. They wouldn't poop on the paving stones. But would they bump into each other? Would they bump into the horses? Probably they would. Maybe there would have to be separate roads for car travel. On the largest piece of paper he could find, he drew a rough map of the city. He figured out where car roads might be: they could cross the city from east to west, and from north to south. He drew a big cross on the map. Some buildings might have to be taken down to make room for the new roads—but that was a fair trade-off. It would mean you could get from, say, the Blue Striped Gate to the Hillside Water Tower in just three or four minutes.

Then you'd want roads out into the countryside, from city to city.

He wrote the names of all seven cities in their approximate locations:

Cliff River City

Sandwater City

Clam Harbor City

Papermill City

Orchard City

Snow Lake City

Steelbright City

Then he drew roads connecting each city to every other city. These would follow the same routes as the train tracks. People might ask, *If you already had the train, why have the cars?* Partly because you could go faster, but a car could go anywhere, not just along tracks. So you'd want to build roads going all different ways so there could be freedom on the land the way there would be, with the Model F, in the sky.

The problem was cutting through the wild lands, the lands that belonged to the plants and animals, the lands where the law said that people must leave no trace and do no harm. But they would just be narrow straight or curved lines through those lands, they wouldn't take up much room. Would they do harm? Keith wasn't sure.

He recalled something he'd thought of after he first saw the Model F: Everybody will want one. It would be the same for cars. Thousands and thousands of people would want one. He tried to imagine the streets of the cities and the roads through the wild lands streaming with cars, and he couldn't do it. Probably his imagination was just not powerful enough. He needed a mind like Malcolm's.

(In fact, Malcolm was indeed thinking thoughts like these, only he was taking them even further. He was thinking of the Multiple Model F, which would be able to fly as many as fifty people at a time. Like Keith, he was entranced by the idea of land travel: cars that would go sixty miles an hour, wide roads where many cars could go in each direction, highways that crossed the whole country. He'd started writing plans for all of these machines, which would be powered, of course, by black dust.)

Keith set aside his project for a while and went downstairs and out to the ball field. He played as hard and fast as ever with Hale and Anders and Pelo and Frank, but he felt separate from them, as if with his secret knowledge he had a foot in another world they didn't belong to. They played until it was almost dark.

When he got home, he found Lulu sitting on the floor, arranging her wooden blocks into a square, and then building the square up higher and higher. When she saw him, she said, "I know this is a boring building. I don't have any good ideas right now."

"Why not?" Lulu often built odd houses and craggy castles.

"I don't know. I'm kind of tired."

"Lulu," Keith said, "do you know what a car is?"

"Yes, I think so. A person could ride in a car on a road, in the old days."

"Wouldn't you love to have one?"

"Why?"

"So you could go anywhere."

"But who would drive it?"

"You would!"

She went back to her blocks, putting on another layer, one by one. "I don't know how. Anyway, I'd rather go on the train, where you don't have to drive."

She's not feeling quite herself, Keith thought. He bent down and whispered to her. "The Model F Grand Introduction is in two weeks and three days. It's going to be so exciting!"

But Lulu just shook her head without saying anything and kept piling on the blocks.

17

Before the Show

Keith was having trouble concentrating. He sat in Ms. Proger's class, listening to her voice go on and on, all on one note, about the work of the Forest Stewards, who grew trees, took care of trees, and cut trees down. There were five hundred Forest Stewards, or maybe five thousand or fifty thousand, Keith had already forgotten the number, and they all wore green-and-brown-striped shirts, and they worked in the vast forests that surrounded the city, keeping everything in order so there were always trees for building and trees for burning, and always new young trees to replace them.

All this was very important, yes. But Keith's mind wandered. He felt as if he should be doing something to get ready, not just sitting in school. Maybe exercises. He put himself on an exercise program over the next few days.

He practiced raising his arms up and down, holding a jar of water in each hand for a weight. He strengthened his legs by going up and down the building's stairs, all three flights, over and over again, and by running downtown and back every day. At meals, he ate as little as possible so he'd be light and could fly higher. His parents noticed.

"What are you training for?" his father asked. "Something special?"

"No, no," Keith said. "I want to be strong, that's all. It feels good."

Lulu noticed, too. She didn't say anything, but she watched him and frowned.

Only about two weeks now before the show. Signs had started appearing all over the city, large painted signs on pieces of wood, nailed to the sides of buildings or hung beside doorways. They said:

INTRODUCING THE MODEL F
NEXT SUNDAY AT FOXBRIDGE FIELD, 12:00.
FREE!
IT'S THE BEGINNING OF A NEW WORLD.

There was no picture of the Model F or of anyone flying, just a painting of the city and forest as if seen from above. Keith had discovered, in his wanderings around the city, twelve of these signs so far. Every time he saw one, a little crowd of people would be gathered around it, and he would join them and listen to what they were saying:

"What's that about?"

"I don't know. These signs are all over."

"A new world? What does that mean?"

"I don't know. Looks interesting."

"What's a Model F?"

"Who knows?"

"Are you going to go?"

"I guess so. Why not?"

"Me too. It's free. What do we have to lose?"

Everywhere it was the same. People were drawn to something new. After all, if it turned out to be silly or boring, they could just walk away. Keith was sure that there would be a big crowd at Foxbridge Field. All their eyes would be on him. Thinking about it made his heartbeat pick up.

On Thursday evening, he asked his parents if they'd seen those signs. They had.

"What kind of gimmick do you think it is?" his father said. "A new world, the signs say. Sounds a bit ridiculous."

His mother said, "You know how merchants are always saying they've got this new soap that's going to change your life, or this new fruit juice, or this new kind of lamp. It's probably something like that."

"I don't know," Keith said. "I have a feeling it's bigger. I want to go, and you should come, too."

"Oh, I don't think so," his father said. "I'm in the midst of a quite exciting new project, a very simple battery, made with ordinary metals, that will produce a fair amount of electricity more or less forever when placed in a current of water!" His father's eyes went wide and his eyebrows went up, as they did when he was excited. "A bit more interesting than this advertising show, don't you think?"

Keith didn't think so. "When you need a break from that project," he said, "come by Foxbridge Field. And see what's going on. Really. I know it's important."

"Why are you so interested in it, Keith?" his mother asked.

"I'm curious! People are talking about it all over the city. Everyone's going to be there!"

"A good reason to stay away, in my opinion," said his father.

"Don't be a grump," his mother said. "Let's at least walk by and see what it is."

Keith couldn't explain, he couldn't beg and plead. But all these weeks, he'd been imagining his parents among the people at the Grand Intro, looking up at their flying son with awe, feeling more proud of him than ever before. They had to come. He'd have to hope curiosity would get them to the field.

The next morning, Lulu said she felt sick and didn't want to go to school. It was her stomach, she said. It had a horrible, swirly feel. Aunt Meg brought her some toast, but she didn't want to eat.

"I'm afraid she's upset about something," Keith's mother said to him. "She doesn't have a fever, just a stomachache. She says her hands are cold."

"Could it be sadness?" Keith asked. "About her parents?"

"Sadness usually makes her cry," his mother said. "This seems more like worry. Do you know if she's having trouble at school?"

"I don't know," Keith said, but he didn't think the problem was school. "I'll go talk to her."

He went in and sat by Lulu, who was curled up under her covers. "I hear you have a stomachache," he said.

"Yes."

"Do you think you ate something bad?"

"No."

"Are you worried about something?"

"Yes."

"Will you tell me what?"

She didn't say anything.

Keith leaned down and spoke very softly. "Is it about the flying?"

She nodded.

"Tell me," Keith said.

"I'm scared. What if something terrible happens when you fly? I couldn't stand it. And then everyone will find out I knew about it all the time and didn't tell, and then it will be my fault that I didn't tell because I should have."

"Nothing terrible is going to happen."

"*You* don't know."

"And anyway, it wouldn't be your fault. You're keeping a promise. That's a good thing."

"I've told all those lies."

"People will understand why. They won't blame you." They'll blame *me,* he thought, for getting you into so much trouble.

"Remember that paper we signed?" Lulu said. "That said we had heard and understood something something?"

"Yes."

"Did you ever read it?"

"No. There wasn't time. I'm sure it's all okay."

Lulu groaned. "Tell me again when the show is."

"It's next Sunday, at Foxbridge Field."

"That place where there's dancing and fiddles sometimes? And races and dog shows?"

"Yes, that place."

"Okay. But I'm not going to school today."

"That's fine." Keith bent down and spoke softly again. "Lulu, thank you for keeping the secret all this time."

"I tried my best," she said. "But I keep feeling like it's going to leak out."

"It won't," said Keith. "I know you can keep it in."

18

Sounds

The girls gathered as usual on the first Tuesday. They walked through the boatyard, past the Curled Iron Gate, and up the alley, where Gloria Garden, who lived downstairs from Amity, was poking among the small shops, muttering to herself, buying things to put in her collecting basket.

Today Mandolyn was carrying the green bag, which held only their feast and a blanket. This day, they needed nothing else.

They were going to do Sounds. When they got to the pond and had laid out their blanket by the big rocks, Mandolyn set the green bag in the shade of a tree. They sat in a line, facing the pond. The water glittered in the sun.

It was Celia who had invented the sounds game. She said, "For the first sound, you need some rocks."

They all stood up and wandered around, looking down, picking up rocks of different sizes and putting them in their pockets, and then they sat where they were before, in a line. "Amity, you first," Celia said. "Throw a rock in the water. Everyone throw in a different way."

Amity threw a rock about the size of a big strawberry. It flew upward and then dropped into the water with a *plunk.* Amity pictured the rock plunging down and hitting the thing at the bottom of the pond.

"Now, you, Mandolyn."

Mandolyn threw her rock out farther than Amity's, and it went *plink* when it hit the water.

"Oates, your turn."

Oates made a high toss, and the sound her rock made was *plop.*

"And Neva."

She stretched her arm out to the side and threw her rock flat toward the pond, and it skidded into the water and skipped three times, making a sound like *spsshhh-spsshhh-spsshhh.*

Lottie threw a narrow rock that went into the water with a whisper, *whssh.*

Last, Celia threw hers—a good big rock, roundish like an orange. It went *ker-plosh* when it hit and sent up a satisfying splash.

"Now," Celia said, "we do the same thing only faster, one after the other, in the same order. Go!"

Plunk-plink-plop spsshhh-spsshhh-spsshhh-whssh-ker-plosh!

"A rock concert!" Celia cheered and clapped her hands, and they all laughed.

"For the next one, you need a blade of grass, a nice sturdy blade about this long." Celia showed a length of about two inches with her fingers.

Everyone wandered about again, finding blades of grass. It was spring, the grass was everywhere, green and sweet-smelling.

When they were sitting in their line again, Celia showed them how to put their hands together with thumbs touching along the sides, and then hold their grass blade between their thumbs. "Now you put your thumbs right up to your mouth and blow." She did this, and after a few tries, she produced an earsplitting bleat, like an angry goat. Everyone did this, and when they all bleated at once, sounding like a *herd* of angry goats, they broke down laughing again.

"Now we do our songs," said Celia. She had told them about this a few days ago. Each person, she said, should make up a small song to sing today. It didn't have to be a masterpiece, just some words in a tune.

Oates went first. She stood up with her back to the pond and sang about butterflies, fluttering her hands like wings.

Neva sang a song with a trotting rhythm about a horse. She did a terrific neigh at the end.

Mandolyn sang with a faraway look about a ship with yellow sails that would carry her out to sea.

Amity sang about rain and wind and thunder, swooping her hair around and letting it fall in front of her face.

Lottie sang a tragic song about an old and wise person who dies.

Celia sang a loud and funny song about ducks, including many quacks.

After each song, they all said how delightful or sad or clever it was, and they talked about how they'd come up with their song, and they all felt good for being smart enough to write a song and brave enough to sing it.

Then it was time to eat. They had black raisin bread, white cheese, tiny green onions, red radishes, and little paper cups of butterscotch pudding. After that, Celia had them stand in a circle, hold hands, and sing a song they all knew—everyone knew it, it was very old, or at least it was sung to a very old tune. They sang in their best voices, all together:

Praise Earth from whom all blessings flow.
Praise sky above and sea below.
Praise creatures great and small between.
Praise darkness, light, and holy green.

They smiled at each other. Mandolyn picked up the empty green bag, and they walked back into the city.

When they got to the Brightspot Apartments, Amity said goodbye and went up the stairs and looked out her window and waved at her friends. This time, she didn't see Keith coming along, so there was no wave. She missed it.

19

Lulu Tells

On the day before the show, after Keith had gone off to play ball, Lulu told Aunt Meg that she couldn't eat her breakfast oatmeal. "Is something wrong with it?" Aunt Meg asked.

"No. I'm just not hungry."

"Do you have a stomachache again?"

"Sort of."

"Poor baby! I'll get you some medicine. Don't worry— it tastes good."

The medicine was warm and tasted like honey and leaves. Aunt Meg stood beside Lulu as she drank it, with an arm over Lulu's shoulder, and somehow Lulu felt tears rising up in her. She laid her head against Aunt Meg's hip, and though she didn't want to, she started to cry.

"Oh, Lulu!" Aunt Meg bent down. "What is it, darling? Is it missing your parents?"

"It's everything." Lulu was now sobbing so hard she could hardly talk. "And there's a secret. Two secrets."

"Secrets? Can you tell me?"

Lulu felt the words come out like an explosion, all blurry. "Keith . . . he flew! When we were at that place, he flew in the sky!"

"Flu?" Aunt Meg said. "You mean he got the flu? What place? I don't understand."

Now that she'd said it out loud, Lulu felt suddenly even more terrible. She shouldn't have said it.

"He didn't get the flu," she said. "He flew. Up in the air. But I can't talk about it. We signed a paper."

Aunt Meg tried to persuade her, but Lulu wouldn't say any more. For the rest of the day—it was Saturday—she stayed in her room, reading a book from the library and drawing pictures of rabbits, which were now her favorite animal. She thought if she could just make it through to-morrow, the day of the show, then everyone would know what was happening and she wouldn't have to worry about that secret anymore. It would all be over with, except for the other secret, which maybe she would never tell anyone.

By afternoon, she was restless. She asked Aunt Meg if she needed anything from the shops, and the answer was yes: bread, tea, and two onions. Lulu put on her jacket because it was chilly outside, and she went downstairs and down the street. She tucked her hands in her pockets, and in the left pocket she felt something crinkly. She pulled it out and looked at it with surprise. She'd forgotten all about it. She'd give it to Keith when she got home.

"Where did you get this?" Keith was smoothing out the wrinkles in the paper.

"I picked it up in Malcolm's office, when we were there. It's just a scrap, I knew he wouldn't miss it."

"But why did you take it?"

Lulu shrugged. "I was mad at him for yelling at me."

The paper was tannish white. It seemed to have been torn in half—one edge was ragged. On it was sticklike writing—clearly Malcolm's. Keith held it under the lamp and made out these words:

Production plan: 10,000 for initial run
Materials for Model F construction:
straps, canisters, dashboard,
steering mechanism, rockets—enough
for 10,000 units
Fuel on hand: 3 tons of powdered coal

There was more, but he stopped reading at that last line. He had tried not to know it before, but now there it was, plain as day: black dust was coal.

"Did you read this?" he asked Lulu.

"Yes," she said. "I can read all the words, but some of

them I don't know how to say. Like these." She pointed at "initial" and "mechanism."

"But do you know what this note means?" Keith asked.

"No," said Lulu. "Except it must be about a rocket. I know that word."

"It's a list of supplies," Keith said. "It's what Malcolm is going to use for the Model F. He wants to make ten thousand of them."

"That's a lot!" Lulu tried to picture ten thousand people flying in the sky, but she couldn't do it. "Is that note helpful to you?"

Keith hardly knew how to answer. He knew already that coal was a fossil fuel. He knew that fossil fuels had—somehow—endangered the world. Now, looking at this bit of paper, he had to recognize that the Model F ran on fossil fuel.

He thought about everything he'd heard: his father saying, about coal, "which of course we do not use." His teacher speaking of something that "nearly destroyed the human race." And the king in Malcolm's book, who said, "The way to stop using fossil fuels is to stop using them."

This little note made it clear: no one should be making a thing like the Model F—certainly not ten thousand of them.

He wished Lulu had never found it.

"Helpful?" he said finally. "I think . . . sort of . . . yes and no."

He must have looked as stunned as he felt. Lulu said, "Are you okay?" and the true answer would have been no. But he said yes, folded the paper and put it in his pocket, and after a while went to bed, where his dilemma shone like a hard light in his head.

The Model F could start the world down a bad path. Should he, Keith, be part of this? No.

On the other hand, did he want to fly? Yes.

But what is more important: doing what you want, or doing what's right?

He let this question fade into the darkness and tried to sleep.

20

Getting There

Sunday morning arrived. Everyone was at the table for breakfast.

"Hey, I just remembered," said Keith, as if he had not been thinking about it most of the night. "That big event at Foxbridge Field is today. It's at noon, I think. Does anyone want to go?"

"I want to," Lulu said.

"No, no," said her aunt Meg. "Not you, Lulu. You're not feeling good. You aren't going anywhere."

"I'm much better." Lulu reached for a biscuit and ate it. "I want to go."

"We'll see," said Aunt Meg.

After breakfast, when Keith and Lulu were off doing other things, Aunt Meg spoke quietly to her husband. "Arthur, Lulu said such a strange thing yesterday. Something about Keith getting the flu, I thought it was, but she said no, she meant he flew, as in flew in the air. She doesn't seem to have a fever, but this seems like a feverish delusion. And then there's her stomachache, too. I think she should stay in bed today, so I can keep an eye on her."

He agreed. "I'll put my project on hold for the moment and go out to the field with you. We can tell her all about it when we get back."

But when Lulu was told of this plan, she was horrified. "No, no, I'm fine," she said. "I'm fine and I want to go. I *have* to go." The thought of missing the whole thing, after all this time and trouble, made her suddenly feel twice as sick as she had before. She couldn't be home in bed while Keith did his flight. Whatever happened, she had to be there. She never should have told a single word of the secret. That was a bad, bad mistake!

She found Keith in his room, lacing up his shoes. She told him what was happening.

He looked up from his shoes with his mouth wide open. "You told her I flew? How could you?"

"I couldn't help it! The secret just came out, but then I clamped down on it. I didn't tell very much. She didn't know what I meant."

"I guess it doesn't matter."

"But now she says I can't go to the show! I have to stay home in bed!"

"No, no, that's terrible. You have to be there. I'll tell her you're fine—I'll tell her right now because I'm on my way out. I've said I'm going to play ball and I'll see them at the field. But really I'm going straight to the field, to get ready."

Lulu looked stricken. "Oh no. You're leaving me?"

"I have to."

"What will I do?"

"Say you made a mistake. Tell them it was just a dream you had about me flying, and now you feel much better."

But Lulu knew she couldn't do that. It would be still another lie on top of the mountain of ones she'd already told. They made her sick, all those lies, as if they were rocks in her stomach.

She'd have to figure out something else.

Keith had closed a door in his mind. All the difficult questions were behind it. He would go to the Grand Introduction as promised, and once he got there, he would either fly or not fly. The right decision would be clear to him, there at the final moment.

At 10:45, he set off on his bike. He rode down to 34th Circle Road, then out past the ironworks and the North Power Station and over the Gray Goose Bridge. He arrived shortly before eleven. Already, a few curious people had come to be in the audience. Keith parked his bike behind the barn and slipped in a back door.

At the same time, Lulu was in bed, and Aunt Meg was sitting in a chair beside her, talking in a soothing way. "A thing that's sad or upsetting," she said, "can sometimes affect a person's body and mind both. You can have a tummy ache because you're upset, and you can have dreams or ideas that aren't exactly real."

"Uh-huh," said Lulu. She pulled the covers up around her and closed her eyes.

"And really," Aunt Meg went on, "a little good medicine and a good sleep can be the right remedy. By the end of the day, I bet you'll feel better in body and mind both."

Lulu didn't answer. She was pretending to be asleep. She pretended very well, but Aunt Meg went on talking. "I'm sure that show wasn't anything you'd have been interested in. Later on, when you've had a good nap, you and I can play checkers or do some drawing."

Lulu could hardly keep still. Time was passing. It must be after eleven by now. She had to get to Foxbridge Field at the beginning of the show or she might miss Keith's flight.

She tried breathing in a slow, even way, like someone who's deeply asleep. She threw in a tiny snore. She heard Aunt Meg whisper, "Ah, very good," and then at last get up and go away.

Lulu waited a second or two and got to work. She tucked some cushions under the covers in the shape of her sleeping self. She pulled on clothes and a sweater, glanced at the clock beside the bed—it was 11:20. She had forty minutes to get to Foxbridge Field by noon. The field was a good distance away, but she could make it; she was fast. She crept out the bedroom door and down the hall to the back outside stairway. In less than thirty seconds, she was down the three flights and onto the street.

She took the same route Keith had, but she had to run because she didn't have a bike. Luckily, she was a good runner. Like a little sewing needle, she wove through the traffic on the street, darting in front of an old woman, around a donkey wagon, jumping over rough spots in the road, not stopping.

By the time she reached the city center, she was panting. She couldn't run at top speed all the way. She would have to hitch a ride. It wasn't hard. She flagged down a woman riding a double bike, who said she was going to the Grand Introduction and Lulu could ride on the seat behind her. To join up with a stranger like this was something you could do in this city, if you were not a shy person, as Lulu was not; strangers weren't dangerous here. Lulu was following what she had always been told: people will do their best to be kind.

They reached the field just before noon. Lulu jumped down from the bike, said thank you for the ride, and made her way into the enormous crowd.

Aunt Meg had discovered Lulu's trick after about twenty minutes. Of course she knew where Lulu had gone, and she realized she couldn't catch up with her. There was no need to. She and Arthur would go to Foxbridge Field, wait for Lulu to show up, and bring her back home, with a little scolding. They would have to hurry, though. They'd need to get there soon so they could find Lulu easily if a big crowd came. "Arthur!" she called. She hustled him down the stairs, telling him what had happened. They hopped on their bikes and got to the field in fifteen minutes.

PART 3

Up in the Air

21

The Grand Introduction

At the end of the field was a barn. It had been a horse barn years ago, but now it was used as a backstage area for Foxbridge Field events. A stage had been built in front of it, and a banner had been nailed to the wall over the stage. It read INTRODUCING THE MODEL F! in tall, bright red letters.

The first people to arrive stood near the stage. Then more and more came and stood behind them until the field was filled, and still people were squeezing in, some sitting on blankets around the edges, some trying to push up closer to the stage, all talking and laughing and waving at each other. This was the biggest gathering the city had seen for a long time. When had there been another crowd this big? The circle dancing? The dog races? No one could remember. It was a happy, lively crowd; even the scoffers, who were sure this was going to be some kind of stupid joke, were having a good time.

Lulu came in at the east edge. She was making her way closer to the stage when she heard her name called out. It was Aunt Meg, who had got there just before, along with Uncle Arthur.

"That was a naughty trick, Lulu," Aunt Meg said.

"I know. But I had to be here. You'll see why."

"Is Keith here?"

"Yes. You'll see."

They found a place where they could see the stage pretty well. Lulu improved her view by climbing a nearby tree.

Lulu was excited and also afraid. She tried not to think of the bad things that might happen. Soon Keith would fly, and all this would be over with.

From her perch in the tree, she saw Amity, who was there with her parents, and with all of her Tuesday friends. They made a little cluster of beauty, over near the poplar trees. She spotted Gloria, too, talking to whoever was standing next to her. She was easy to spot—no one else had such an enormous frizz of white hair.

What was Keith doing right now? Lulu wondered. How was he feeling?

Keith was at the moment standing in one of the old horse stalls in the barn, feeling sweaty and cold. He was wearing a red flight suit; on the front was an F made of shiny silver cloth. On his feet were the newest shoes, also of silver cloth, fastened with red shoelaces. A full-length mirror leaned against one of the boxes. When he saw himself in it, he thought he looked wonderful, though there was a small part of him that thought he looked foolish.

Stacked around the edges of the barn were dozens of boxes, each one containing, Keith had been told, equipment for a complete Model F, plus some extra fuel canisters. Malcolm had explained that after the demonstration people from the audience would swarm forward, eager to buy their own Model Fs, and Dodge and Roam would sell them. "The demand will be huge," Malcolm said, "so huge that if anyone tries to stop us, the citizens will rise in revolt. Old ways will be thrown on the scrap heap. New ways will triumph!"

Preparations were in high gear. Malcolm and his team strode about, unpacking crates, making notes on clipboards, and talking in short bits:

"Canisters ready?"

"Yeah, all ready."

"Get me that box over there."

"Where's the kid?"

"Right there."

"Time?"

"Fourteen minutes to go."

Malcolm came and stood before him. He had actually

combed his hair today and put some sort of grease on it so it swept backward and stayed there. He was wearing a blue long-sleeved top that fitted him tightly. His belly made a slight bulge beneath it, but otherwise he looked trim and vigorous. "You look great," he said to Keith. "You know the plan: I'll go out and do my speech and get the crowd excited; then I'll introduce you, and the music will start, and you'll go up. Are you ready?"

"I think so."

Malcolm raised his eyebrows. "What's not ready? We'll fix it."

"It's nothing. Just feeling a little nervous." Keith put a hand on his stomach, which was doing flips. But it wasn't because he was afraid of flying or of people watching him. It was because the time had come for him to say what he was going to say to Malcolm.

"Understandable," said Malcolm. "A thousand people out there. An extraordinary moment. But nervousness is bad for flying." He took Keith by the shoulders and looked him straight in the eye. "You need to calm down. As soon as you're up, you will."

At that moment, Keith could see the words in his head, clear as if they were written in ink: *I think Project F is a step in the wrong direction, and probably against the law, and I don't want to be part of it.*

Those were the words he should say.

But he didn't say them. Instead, in a great rush, other

words came out of his mouth. "Yes, you're right, I'm a little nervous, but not very. Really not much at all. I'll be fine." He felt his voice getting loud and breathless. "I want to fly, and I *will* fly, and I'll be terrific!"

Malcolm grinned and leaned slightly away from Keith, as if his words had been a strong wind. "That's the spirit!" he said. "That's what I like to hear! You're a hundred percent in, then. Right?"

"Right!" said Keith, and a feeling of sickness flooded through him and then was gone.

"Good boy," said Malcolm. "The world changes today, and"—he smiled and winked—"our fortunes change, too."

Keith watched him stride among the men of the team, with a grin or a pat for all of them. He heard Malcolm say the words "change the world" over and over.

But the words that struck him at that moment were the other ones: "Our fortunes change, too." Of course. It wasn't just that flying was wonderful and would give people freedom. It was also that flying was going to make Malcolm a lot of money. There was nothing wrong with making money. Still, the sick feeling stirred again.

"Ten minutes!" shouted Dodge.

Keith pressed his hands against his stomach and closed his eyes and took a deep, shuddering breath. When he looked up, he saw that Malcolm was watching him. He was at the back of the tent, huddling with Dodge and Roam. They were talking in low voices. Keith saw Dodge look his

171

way and nod. Malcolm went behind a curtain into a space that served as a dressing room.

"Five minutes," said Roam, trotting around to everyone.

Dodge came up to Keith. "Last-minute change," he said. "I'll be starting the show instead of Malcolm."

"You will? Why?"

"He'll come out later," Dodge said, and he hurried away before Keith could ask any more.

The five minutes passed. Dodge stepped out on the stage, and Keith listened as he shouted out to the crowd:

"Greetings, everyone! Greetings!" He had to shout it several times before the crowd settled down and paid attention. "You've come to the right place on the right day to see something amazing, something that will astound and delight you. And I want you to know: this is not just a show. You'll see something you can do, too, every one of you. We are introducing a miraculous device that will change the way you live. It's called the Model F."

He paused, and Keith could hear the crowd murmuring. Then a sudden hush—Dodge had held up a hand.

"I want to introduce two people who will show you what the Model F can do."

Two? The plan had been for him to fly alone.

"First: Keith Arlo! Come on out, Keith!"

Keith stepped up onto the stage. He felt as if a million lights were shining at him—at his red outfit and his silver shoes, at the equipment he was wearing. His mother was out there in that crowd—maybe even his father, if he'd changed his mind. And of course Lulu was there, and maybe his friends from school, and maybe his teachers. He raised his arms in the way he'd practiced, and there was a roar from the crowd and some cries of "Keith! It's Keith!"

Dodge was shouting again. "And now," he cried, "the genius behind it all! Meet Malcolm Quinsmith!"

Malcolm appeared, strode onto the stage, and stood beside Keith, with his arms raised in the same way. He, too, was wearing a flying suit; he, too, had on all the equipment.

The crowd clapped. While Dodge went on about the history of the project and its bright future, while he told the crowd that the F in Model F stood for freedom, Malcolm spoke in a hoarse, urgent whisper to Keith. "Not letting you do this alone," he said. "If you're nervous even a tiny bit, you need a backup. Anyhow, I realized: this is *my* project, it's the big moment, and *I need to be up there*." He took hold of Keith's shoulder, his fingers digging in hard, and turned him so they were facing each other. "F for flight," he said. "F for freedom, F for our fortunes, F for the great future! We'll show the world the way forward!"

Keith saw the truth of Malcolm then, in his piercing, burning gaze: yes, he was a genius—but the kind who would set the world on fire to get what he wanted.

It was too late now to back out.

Dodge was holding up a flaming torch—some shrieks from the crowd—and bending to light the rockets on Keith's legs. The rockets roared. It was time to go. Keith turned the handle and began to rise.

Seconds later, he heard the roar of rockets again and knew Malcolm was close behind. So he turned up the power and rose higher. He would get away from Malcolm, as far away as he could. He was angry at Malcolm, and angry at himself, and his anger was like an extra boost.

Below, the people in the crowd had all tipped their heads back and were staring upward and crying out "ooooh" and "aaaah." Keith flew higher, and their voices grew faint. The field was a faraway rectangle. He was above the leafy tops of the trees now, and above the roofs of the highest buildings, nothing but sky above him, and the only sound the hissing and growling of his engines. He spread his arms, tipped and turned, and looked down to see Malcolm speeding up toward him. Again, he felt the surge of anger, and also determination. Now that he was doing this, he would do it *right*, he would do it *best*. He swooped to the east, out toward the river, and then back again, and then to the north toward the cornfields and back, and suddenly there was Malcolm right below his shoes, with his eyes wide and his arms reaching, as if to grab Keith's feet. "Slow down," Malcolm called, but Keith wasn't going to slow down. With a shot of power, he went straight up, leaving yards of empty space between them.

It had crossed his mind, when he first took off, to fly badly on purpose, to show people that flying was wrong. But he couldn't help it: he flew beautifully. He sailed in great loops over the people below, sloped downward and climbed up, did a spin, did a backflip, and felt that he was king of the world. Green stretched to the west and north, the busy, multicolored city below, the curved blue line of the river to the east—how beautiful it all was, how perfect! A flock of tiny birds appeared, whisked past him, and was gone.

Where was Malcolm? He was far below, but he was climbing. His rockets pulsed, *r-r-r-r, r-r-r-r,* and with each pulse he came closer, and then Keith could see his face, which wore an expression of fury. He understood at once: Malcolm wanted to be first and highest. It was *his* project! He should be the star!

Keith pulled up top speed and aimed for the sun.

Malcolm followed. The higher Keith flew, the more desperately Malcolm came after him. But he seemed to have forgotten that because of his greater weight, he couldn't fly for as long as Keith. His fuel would begin to run out, and in fact, Keith could tell from the sputtering roars that it was running out now.

Malcolm seemed not to notice. He came closer, his jaw clenched tight, and he edged past Keith without speaking to him and kept on going, though his rockets were gasping. Keith watched with growing terror. He was looking up now at Malcolm, who flew across the brightness of the sun, flung his arms up, and let out a long howl, maybe of triumph, maybe of rage.

Then, with two threads of smoke, his rockets went silent, and Malcolm began to fall.

22

Crash Landing

Keith had enough fuel left to make an awkward, stumbling landing at the edge of the field. He ended up on his knees, breathing hard, his eyes fixed on the ground. Sparks from his engines ignited a fire in the grass. Flames spread out around his body, making a black circle, but they didn't go far; people rushed in to stamp them out.

He heard his name called, and within a minute, his parents were there bending over him, and Lulu was crying, "Keith, Keith! Are you alive?"

He got to his feet. Nothing seemed broken. He unstrapped the Model F and laid it on the ground. "What happened to Malcolm?" he said.

It was Lulu who answered. "He banged into a tree. The branch broke. I couldn't see where he fell."

Keith turned and scanned the crowd. He could see a

bunch of people gathered tightly together, and arms up and waving as if calling for help. That must be where Malcolm was.

"I have to find him," he said, and he broke away from his startled parents, pushed into the mass of people, and made his way to where he thought he'd find Malcolm.

All around him, he heard talk about what had just happened. "So terrible!" "What an insane idea—to fly!" "Ridiculous!" "But how wonderful, when the boy did it." "Wouldn't you love to do that?" "The machine doesn't work, though." "It's dangerous." "But it's new; it's still being refined. Later versions will work better." "No, no, I'd never try it."

Keith heard all this as if he were moving through a buzzing cloud of insects. Across the field, in the midst of the bunch of people, was Malcolm, lying in a twisted way, not moving, with his Model F equipment fallen half off him, half-broken. "Let me through," Keith said, and seeing his red suit, the others made space.

"He's unconscious," someone said, "but alive. The doctors are coming."

Keith knelt down next to Malcolm, whose eyes were closed. His red suit was ripped at the shoulder, and there was a cut on his face, bleeding down into his ear. Keith couldn't tell if any of his bones were broken. He unstrapped the parts of the Model F as well as he could.

Someone tapped him on the shoulder and said, "It was great the way you flew."

"Doctor coming!" he heard, and the crowd parted, and four people in the blue clothes of doctors came and bent over Malcolm and checked his pulse and his breathing and lifted his eyelids and listened to his heart. They unfolded a stretcher and lifted him onto it, and before long, they had laid him in a long, slim horse cart and carried him away.

"I want to fly like you," said a little girl, tugging on Keith's arm.

"Does it take a lot of practice?"

"Will the machine be for sale soon?"

"You could have killed yourself. I wouldn't touch that thing."

"No, I want one, I want one."

Because of the accident, there wasn't the huge surge of customers flocking to buy the Model F that Malcolm had hoped for, the surge that would have proved how extremely popular and valuable this new technology was, overcoming the objections of those who wished to stop it. Still, a few people ran to the barn after the sudden end of the Grand Intro, wanting a Model F for themselves, and Dodge and Roam sold eight of them.

All Keith wanted was to get away. He crossed the field and found his parents waiting for him. They said nothing; neither did he. They walked through the city toward home.

He didn't know what to think. All he knew was that he had just had the most thrilling and the most terrible experience of his life, both at once, and from it he had learned a truth: What you know is best can be easily swept aside by what you want.

When they got home, they sat together at the table, all four of them. "Now," said Keith's father, "you must tell us how all this came about."

Keith did. He told them everything, from the switched blue bags to the final flight.

"Did you not remember what I said to you at the train station?" his father asked.

"Yes. You said don't get caught up in anything."

"But you did."

"I thought it would be easy, and interesting. Return the bag, find out about the project, come home."

"But you kept going with it. You *joined* the project."

"I did."

"And," said Keith's mother, "you brought *Lulu* into it. You put her in *danger!*"

"No," said Lulu. "There wasn't danger to me. Except I had to tell lies."

"KEITH!" his mother cried, flinging her hands out. "This is by far the most reckless, dangerous, deceptive thing you have ever done! And stupid! What were you thinking?"

There was silence for a moment. Keith stared down at a spot of sunlight on the table. He felt small. "I thought it would be good for the world," he said. "It was such a wonderful thing, flying. It would be freedom for everyone. I wanted to be part of it."

His father shook his head slowly back and forth, as if he couldn't comprehend his son's foolishness. "It may be hard for us to trust you ever again."

Keith didn't know what to say. He was quiet for a while. Finally he said, "What did you think of my flying?"

His mother sighed. "Astounding," she said. "Horrifying."

"Yes," his father said. "It *was* astounding. It did take some courage, I suppose."

Lulu spoke up. "I saw Keith fly the first time! It was thrilling! He was high up, like a bird!"

Both Keith's mother and father allowed themselves to imagine, just for a second, how wonderful it would be to fly and why Keith was so tempted to do it.

"What powered that machine?" his father asked.

Keith had been dreading this question. "I didn't know, at the time," he said. "Remember when I asked you about black dust? It was that. It was coal dust."

His father's eyes went wide. His mother leaned her head into her hand and said, "Oh no."

"You mean," said Keith's father, "this man wanted to bring back fossil fuels? Which are against the law because

181

using them nearly wrecked human civilization and all life on the planet?"

Keith said, "I didn't exactly know that." His shoulders slumped, and his face grew hot.

"I'm afraid you could be in serious trouble," said his father. "I'm not sure if there's still the same penalty for breaking that law. It's been so long since anyone did. But if it is the same, then—"

At that moment, footsteps sounded on the stairs, and someone knocked loudly on the front door.

23

Consequences

When Keith's father opened the door, two people stepped inside, a man and a woman, both wearing dark blue suits with a small silver badge on the pocket.

"Good evening," said the woman. "We're from the Department of Energy. Investigators. We're looking for Keith Arlo."

Keith's heart plunged into his stomach. He stood up and faced the officers. "I'm Keith," he said.

"I'm Officer Shirley," said the woman. She had hair like a small dark cloud. "This is Officer Clyde." He had pink cheeks, and his ears stuck out from his head.

Keith's father, gesturing toward the kitchen, said, "Please. Come and sit down. We must talk about this." He brought in two more chairs, and everyone sat around the table.

Officer Shirley began. She explained that they'd known right away that the Model F must be running on some sort of fossil fuel, and as soon as they examined it, they could see that it was. "As you know, this is a violation of the law," she said. Her steady brown eyes were trained on Keith.

"Yes," he said. "I know now."

"There is a punishment for using or promoting these fuels," Officer Clyde said.

"It is quite severe," said Officer Shirley, "to suit the seriousness of the crime."

They paused, looking at Keith, whose heart was pounding. "Is it jail?" His voice croaked, caught in his throat.

"No," said Officer Clyde. "It is banishment. Complete and permanent."

Keith's mother gasped. His father sighed and murmured, "Yes, I was right."

"But what does that mean?" Keith cried. "What is banishment?"

"To be banished is to be sent away," said Officer Clyde, speaking in a solemn, important-sounding voice. "Take the example of Malcolm Quinsmith. He is currently in the hospital, unconscious, having banged his head quite hard on a branch as he fell. He has two broken legs and several broken ribs. If he recovers, he will be banished from Cliff River City. That is, he will have to leave here and go to another city to live. He can never come back."

Keith took a breath, trying to find his voice. "And . . . ," he said, "this could happen to me?"

"Potentially," said Officer Clyde.

Keith's mother slapped the table, making the cups jump. "No!" she cried. "Our son, sent away? I won't allow it!"

"I will go with him!" Lulu said. She slapped her hand on the table, too.

"No, no, that would make it even worse!" Keith's mother, wild-eyed, stood halfway up from her chair.

"If I might continue," said Officer Clyde.

She sat down, her hands gripped together.

Officer Clyde resumed. "We have many questions about Mr. Quinsmith's business. His partners, whoever they were, seem to have vanished. No one we spoke to knew anything about them. Many people, however, knew *you*"—he pointed at Keith—"and knew where you lived. That's why we're here."

"To banish me," said Keith.

"Absolutely not!" cried Keith's mother, jumping up again.

"We're not sure yet." Officer Clyde cleared his throat loudly. "First, we'd like to ask you some questions, Keith."

Keith nodded.

"What was your reason for taking part in Project F?"

"To fly," Keith said.

"That is," said Officer Shirley, "to advertise the flying machine? To make people want to buy it?"

"Yes, but mainly, to try it myself."

She pulled a notebook from her pocket and jotted something down on it. "Did you know what fuel it used?"

"No," Keith said. "Or—not until just before the Grand Introduction."

"I see." She made another note.

"He is only thirteen," his mother said, even though she knew Keith's fourteenth birthday was in two and a half weeks.

Officer Shirley agreed to take Keith's youth into account. "We could allow his family to go with him into his banishment," she said.

Keith's father and mother exchanged looks. What about their jobs and their home and everything that connected them to this place where they'd always lived? What about Lulu and her school and her friends?

Keith saw that he had ruined everything—his family's lives, not just his own.

Officer Shirley asked Keith a few more questions, and then she said, "Will you excuse us for a moment? Officer Clyde and I need to speak privately."

It would have been a good moment for Keith's mother to make tea and bring out some crackers, but they were all too nervous for that. After several minutes, the investigators came back.

"Technically," Officer Shirley said, "Keith should be banished for his part in Project F, which he knew was against the law—at least he knew it at the last minute."

Keith felt doom closing in on him.

"However," Officer Clyde went on, "we would like to propose a bargain. We don't know how or where this project came to be. All its partners have disappeared. Until Malcolm wakes up—which could be never—Keith is the only one who can answer our questions."

"Not the *only* one," said Lulu. "I was there, too."

The officers were astonished. "Wonderful!" said Officer Shirley. "Then we'd like to ask you questions, too. For help from both of you, we could cancel Keith's banishment. What do you say?"

"Of course!" said Keith, feeling suddenly lighter than air, and Lulu said, "I will!" and relief and joy filled the room.

Not only did Keith and Lulu answer all the officers' questions, they made a trip on the train together, the four of them, to Graves Mountain. Keith showed them Malcolm's office, where they shuffled through his papers, making notes, for quite a while. Then he led them into the tunnel that went into the mountain behind the building, and with some effort, Officer Shirley wrenched open the large doors with the flying purple F above them. Keith said he'd heard a *clickety-clack* sound from behind them, like a string of little train cars on a track, and indeed that was what they saw—a rail line, left from the long-ago days when Graves Mountain had been a coal-mining town. They ventured some distance into the dark mouth of the mine, and in the light of the officers' flashlights, they saw pickaxes and shovels and pieces of black rock—clear evidence that Malcolm had had teams of miners down there, hacking at a seam of coal and loading the chunks into bucket-like train cars, which brought them up to headquarters, where they were pounded into the dust that became the Model F's fuel.

In the days after this trip, when Keith and Lulu were back home, the investigators sent workers to Graves Mountain. The workers blocked the mine with stones. They took down the buildings, and a freight train carried their remains to Demo Depot #17 East, where they joined the mountain of things the world could no longer use.

24

Malcolm's Fate

After a couple of weeks, the investigators informed the Arlo family that Malcolm had recovered slightly and was able to talk. Keith decided to visit him in the hospital. He was a little afraid of doing this; he and Malcolm were not exactly friends. But Malcolm was important to him. Malcolm had given him the most wonderful experience of his life—flying—and the harshest lesson. It seemed wrong to let him go away to another city forever without a word.

He told his parents he was going. He told Lulu, too, and asked if she'd like to come along. She looked into the air for a moment and rubbed her chin, thinking. "I don't really like him," she said. "But I'm sort of curious."

So they went together on a Saturday morning. It was a glorious summer day. Banners and laundry and people's bright-colored clothes fluttered in the breeze. Everyone seemed in a lively mood; even the dogs were especially frisky, and the whinnying of the horses was like laughter. Keith bought lemonade for both of them, and they drank it as they walked the ten blocks to the hospital.

Inside was a lobby with a desk adorned by a pot of yellow tulips. A young man sat at the desk, and Keith asked him Malcolm's room number. "Down that hall," the man said, pointing. "Number 107."

The door of 107 stood open. Keith knocked on it, received no answer, and went in with Lulu behind him.

There was Malcolm, lying under a white sheet, with his head on a white pillow, and his eyes closed. His hair was spread out like a ragged dark sunflower around his face. He was snoring softly.

"Should we wake him up?" Lulu whispered.

Keith nodded. He put a hand on Malcolm's arm.

Malcolm's eyes shot open. He stared at Keith for a second. Then he closed his eyes again. "You," he said.

"Yes," said Keith. "I came to see how you are."

"Alive," said Malcolm without opening his eyes. "No thanks to you."

"I'm here, too," said Lulu.

"Great," Malcolm said. He sounded very tired.

"Malcolm, please look at me," Keith said. "I want to talk about what happened."

"I don't," Malcolm said, with his eyes still closed. "*You* talk, if you have to."

"I know you've been badly injured," Keith said, "and I'm sorry you were, and I hope you get better soon."

"Mm-hmm," said Malcolm.

"And I have some questions."

Malcolm opened his eyes. "Go on."

"Why did you decide to fly that day? At the Grand Intro?"

"I wanted to."

"But we'd planned that I would fly by myself."

"I changed my mind, that's all. At the last minute. I saw you all ready to go, and I thought, Of *course* I have to fly. It's my project!" He thumped his fist weakly on the bed.

"And you didn't think you might be too heavy?"

"No. I didn't think about it."

"You flew all the way up to the sun," said Lulu.

"That's right." Malcolm turned his face toward the wall. "This visit is over," he said.

"But there's one more thing." This was what Keith most wanted to know.

Malcolm made a grumpy sound.

"Project F was against the law. Did you know that?"

"Of course I knew that."

"And you didn't care?"

Malcolm turned back toward Keith and glared at him. "Remember about freedom? About progress, and moving forward? *That's* what people care about. There are more important things than obeying a law."

Lulu, tired of this angry talking, had gone to stand at the window. "Look," she said, pointing upward. "A kite!"

They all looked up. Someone was standing on a roof-top, flying a bright red kite that was so high in the sky it was just a dot. For a moment, they all watched it dart and swoop.

Keith turned back to Malcolm. "What will you do now?"

"I am banished," Malcolm said. "They're sending me to Steelbright City. I'll continue my work; I'm not giving up. Maybe the people there aren't as backward as the ones here."

"Thank you for the chance to fly," Keith said. "I loved it."

"I'm glad I got to see it," said Lulu.

"But maybe people aren't meant to fly," Keith said. "At least not that way."

"Only birds and kites should fly," Lulu said. "And bees."

Malcolm closed his eyes again and pulled the covers up around his neck. "Goodbye," he said. "I'll send you a postcard."

He never did. He was in the hospital for several weeks, where he was given medicine for pain and medicine for treating infections. (Both were among the Things of Great Value saved over the centuries from ancient times.) Still, his injuries healed only partly, leaving him unable to walk. When he got stronger, hospital workers helped him onto the Monday-morning northbound train to Steelbright City, and there he roamed the streets in his wheelchair, talking to anyone who would listen about the need to return to fossil fuels. The speed! The power! The progress for human kind! Most people didn't want to listen.

Dodge and Roam, when they saw that the Grand Introduction was a catastrophe, had understood what could happen to them, and they made for the river as fast as possible and rode a fishing boat to the seacoast. There they signed on as workers on a sailing ship bound for Spain and were not seen again in Cliff River City.

All the others who had worked on Project F also managed to disappear. The miners, who had never much liked hacking out coal in a dark tunnel, moved to Sandwater City and spent the rest of their lives enjoying the sun.

25

Endings and Beginnings

Keith was so grateful not to be banished that he decided to devote himself to school, at least for a while. He would pay close attention and strive to become less ignorant. This turned out to be easy. Ms. Proger had decided she'd rather teach the littlest students, who didn't ask as many hard questions, and so Keith had a new history teacher. He was a wild-haired man named Alf Redondo, who was so fascinated by what he taught, and taught it with such vigor and humor, that Keith had no trouble paying attention.

He learned all he should have known before about the Sudden Rise and the Sudden Fall. One day, Mr. Redondo took a thick pencil and drew a line all the way across the back wall. "Here's human history," he said. "About two hundred thousand years." He stood close to the end of the line and drew a tiny peak.

————————————————————————/\———————

"That's when we started using fossil fuels. Sudden Rise. Terrific power! Fabulous luxury lifestyle! Amazing speed! A few hundred years later—Sudden Fall. Turns out the luxury lifestyle was wrecking the planet. It took a major catastrophe to turn that around."

Keith glanced out the classroom window. One of the few Model Fs that Dodge and Roam had managed to sell before fleeing was zooming in the sky, making its growling, buzzing noise. He thought it might be the last one. The others had been confiscated as soon as they were found. Watching the flier gave Keith a dark feeling. He no longer wished to be flying himself.

Mr. Redondo noticed it, too. "Some people," he said, "long to take up that way of living again."

Keith felt faces turning toward him, and his own face went hot.

"Don't blame Keith!" cried Mr. Redondo. "Come on, admit it—if you were given the chance to fly, how many of you would do it? Hands in the air."

Most of the hands went up. Mr. Redondo's did, too.

"Yes! So much about that time was wonderful—beyond

wonderful! But the cost of living that way was too high. The older you get, the more you'll learn about what almost happened to our world. You'll understand it deeply, in here." He thumped his heart. "You'll know we can never go that way again."

One day, when Lulu was on her way down the stairs, she ran into Gloria coming up from the street. Gloria didn't seem to be mad at her. She was carrying a big cloth bag so full there were bulges all over it. She said, "Hello, little one, so nice to see you, where are you off to?"

Lulu said she was going to buy some oranges at the store. "How is your house?" she asked.

"My house? My house is fine, I'm getting it back the way I like it."

"You are?" Lulu said, with a pang of dread. "May I come in and visit sometime?"

"I don't think so," said Gloria. "You were the one who got people to take away my belongings. You might do the same again." She grinned in a teasing way, but Lulu could tell she was serious. It worried her. When she got back home, she told Aunt Meg that Gloria was collecting again and wouldn't let her in.

"Hmm," said Aunt Meg. "That's a problem."

Lulu thought about it, and after a few days, she came

197

up with a solution. She told Aunt Meg, who thought it was a good idea. That afternoon, they baked a batch of walnut muffins and put them on a wide plate. Lulu took them downstairs and knocked on Gloria's door.

Gloria opened the door a tiny crack and peered out. "Oh, little Lulu," she said. "Hello."

"I thought you might like these," Lulu said. "May I bring them in?"

Gloria hesitated.

"Or I can just hand you this plate."

"I think that's a better idea, just in case, dear, because you know what happened before, and I wouldn't want—"

Lulu interrupted. "Here you go," she said. She nudged the door with her foot until there was enough space to fit the wide plate through. It took several seconds for Gloria to bend down and get a grip on the plate and stand up again, and during those seconds, Lulu took a good look at the room. Definitely cluttered—many baskets, bags, and boxes everywhere—but not nearly as bad as before.

"Thank you, thank you!" Gloria said. "These will be delicious, I don't have time to bake muffins these days, I'm so busy with—"

"You're welcome!" said Lulu.

Back upstairs, she reported to Aunt Meg, and they agreed that this was a good way to keep an eye on Gloria. The Muffin Monitoring System, they could call it. Lulu was pleased.

Almost everything seemed better now that the flying was over and that secret was out. But the other secret was still in her, like a drop of poison. She knew she could never tell it. She thought she would have to carry it always, until one afternoon when she was in the kitchen with Aunt Meg, shelling peas. Aunt Meg was talking about her sister— that is, Lulu's mother, Alice, who drowned. "She was such a cheery person," she said. "We always had a good time. We used to shell peas together or peel potatoes or cut out cherry pits, and we'd tell each other jokes while we did it and laugh our heads off. Did you laugh with your mother, Lulu?"

Lulu just nodded, not smiling.

"I miss her," Aunt Meg went on. "She had such a lot of energy, and she was smart and feisty and fun to talk with. You are like her, Lulu."

"No," Lulu said, with a dark look. "Not as good."

"Why do you say that? Of course you're good!"

Lulu could feel the dangerous tightening of her throat, and the dangerous tears coming up. She saw that Aunt Meg knew what she was feeling, and she turned her face away.

"Tell me what the trouble is," Aunt Meg said. It was not a demand. Her voice was so, so kind, and that put Lulu right on the brink of telling. She squeezed her eyes shut, but it didn't help. The words began to come out.

"It was on the beach," she said.

"Yes?" said Aunt Meg encouragingly.

Lulu went on very fast then in a voice that was mostly sobs. "I was building a sandcastle, and my mother was helping me, but she knocked down part of it accidentally, it was the tower, it was the best part, and I got so mad at her I said angry words."

"What words?" Aunt Meg asked.

"I said quit helping me, you're no good at it, you make it worse. Let *me* do it by myself. Go away. Go out there and go swimming." Lulu said these words just as she'd said them then: in a loud, furious voice. She flung her hand outward, as she had once flung it toward the sea.

"And what happened?"

"She went out there, and she got caught in the wave. And my father went in to save her, and . . ."

She couldn't say any more, she could only cry.

"Oh," said Aunt Meg, putting her arms around Lulu.

"And then," Lulu cried, "they were swept away! Both of them!"

"It wasn't your fault," Aunt Meg said.

"It was! If I hadn't said that—"

"No, no." Aunt Meg hugged Lulu close. "It was an accident. Your mother loved swimming. She would have gone in sooner or later, no matter what you said."

"I don't know," said Lulu.

"I do. I know for sure. It was a terrible accident, and you didn't cause it." She let go of Lulu, took a hanky from her pocket, and wiped Lulu's eyes and nose. "Do you feel better?" she asked.

Lulu felt shaky. She couldn't tell if she felt better. She sat there with Aunt Meg for a while, and they looked out the window at the big clouds sailing slowly by. "That smaller one looks like a squirrel," Aunt Meg said.

"More like a kangaroo," said Lulu.

They talked about the clouds, and then they finished shelling peas. They didn't say any more about the secret Lulu had told, and that was all right. Lulu had said all she needed to. By dinnertime, she felt a bit better.

In the days that followed, she began to realize that the dark spot of poison was fading. Summer had come, and all the joys that go with it, and that helped. Lulu rode her bike around the neighborhood and played hide-and-seek after school with friends and drew pictures of flowers and animals. It took a while for the dark spot to disappear completely, but it did. There was still the sadness of missing her parents; that never went away. But getting rid of the secret made her feel clean and free.

Keith, however, felt a hole in his life now that the flying project was over. How could he ever have another adventure as great as flying? He wasn't sure what he should do with himself. When he wasn't at school or playing ball, he spent a lot of time wandering around the city, especially in the streets and courtyards of the city center, where things were always happening.

It was on one of these wanderings that he saw someone he recognized—a man sitting on a bench, tossing crumbs to the pigeons. He was sure it was the same man. How could there be two with that huge, unruly beard, that droopy-brimmed leather hat, that red bandanna, and the great clumpy boots on his stretched-out legs? He'd seen him only once, on his first train trip, but it had to be him.

Keith sat down on the bench next to this stranger. "Hello," he said. "I remember you from the train."

The man turned toward him, and once again, there were the squinched eyes and the smile within the whiskers.

"You saw me just for a second," Keith said. "You wouldn't remember me. I'm Keith Arlo."

"Badger Borski," the man said. "Just off a train myself."

"Where have you been?"

"Oh, up north this time. Lakes, mountains, eagles, bears. It was great. Now I'm back for a spell of city life. I'll be looking for a place to live. Do you know of any?"

Of course Keith did.

A week later, after some meetings with the people of the Brightspot Apartments, Badger Borski moved into the empty apartment on the third floor. Keith's parents and Gloria and the Wings had been alarmed by his appearance at first, but as soon as they began talking, they saw his humor and kindness, and they welcomed him.

Keith and Lulu helped him bring his things up the stairs. "This room was mine," Lulu said, leading him to it. "You should sleep here."

"I will, then," said Badger.

It was the beginning of a new life for Keith. Often in the evenings, he would go downstairs, and he and Badger would sit by the fire and talk. Badger lived for adventure. His habit was to take the train to places he'd never been and then get off and walk into the forest, or the desert, or the mountains, or whatever happened to be there. He told Keith his stories—about climbing to great heights on mountainsides, sliding across frozen lakes, discovering deep caves where blind fish lived in pools, running rapids on a log, rescuing a bear cub stranded on a cliff ledge, and exploring ruins from before the Sudden Fall. "It's all out there," he said. "Places you've never been, things you've never seen, all within walking distance."

When Keith told him about *his* big adventure, flying with the Model F, Badger listened with interest and said how exciting that must have been. But he had little praise for Malcolm. "Buzzing around the sky in a machine," he said, shaking his head. "Sometimes people have such small dreams."

It wasn't long before Keith began going with Badger

on an adventure now and then, and a few years later, he began setting out on adventures of his own, often with his friend Frank. On one of these adventures, in a vast wilderness of high rocks and steep brown hillsides, he saw the bird he'd imagined on that first train ride—a condor, its huge wings outspread, gliding high in the air, silent and majestic.

26

The Thing in the Pond

After the disastrous Model F Grand Introduction, another first Tuesday came along. Amity, who had a truly terrific idea for this month's gathering, asked the girls if she could bring Keith and Lulu with her, and they all said yes.

Keith was surprised to be invited, and pleased, and Lulu was purely thrilled.

"I've seen those girls going off on their trips," she told Keith. "They look so happy and beautiful."

"Why do you think they're inviting us this time?" Keith asked.

"I don't know. We'll go, won't we?"

"Yes. We will."

On Tuesday, in the early afternoon, they set out. It was a warm day, almost hot. Amity had changed her favorite colors now. They were blue and green, with touches of white. She wore her blue dress that had no waist and a green-and-white-striped shirt, very loose, that flew out at the sides as she walked. She had put her hair up on her head in a tight bun. She carried a small white bag. Oates carried the bag with the feast and the picnic cloth.

"This is Keith," Amity said when all the girls were there. She didn't need to say it; they all knew who he was. "And this is Lulu. They are my neighbors."

They all greeted the newcomers, and Mandolyn said, "We have a Mystery Trip today. Usually we plan what we're going to do, but today Amity has an idea, and she hasn't told us what it is."

"I like a mystery," Lulu said, and Keith said a mystery was fine with him, too.

They went as they always did, down by the boat docks, up through the fruit market, past the White Wood Gate and the Old Red Gate, to the stump where they turned left toward the pond. Keith had never come this way before. He hadn't known there was a pond nearby.

The water in the pond was very still, a bluish green, reflecting the white trunks of the trees nearby. Oates spread out the cloth, and they all sat down on it, facing Amity. Keith had no idea what the mystery was going to be, but he was looking forward to the feast.

"I'll be right back," Amity said. She took her white bag and walked a little way into the woods, where she changed into her swimming slip. When she came back, Lulu looked at her and cried, "We're going swimming!"

"No," said Amity. "Only me. Remember I've said there's something at the bottom of the pond? Today we're going to get it out."

Gleeful shouts from the girls, except Oates, who said she was afraid the thing might be alive and bite.

"It's not alive, I know that," Amity said. "I'm pretty sure it's quite big and heavy. But I don't know what it is."

Keith was intrigued. "I'll help," he said.

"Everyone will help."

Amity explained her plan. This took a while; it was fairly complicated, and there were many questions. Keith thought of a few things that could go wrong, but he didn't say any of them. Probably Amity had already thought of them. Her idea was clever, and it might very well work.

When she was finished, Amity looked around at all the faces. "Shall we do it?"

Everyone said yes.

Amity opened her bag and took out a coil of rope—not thick heavy rope, but sturdy and long. On one end of it she had tied a metal hook, about the size of a hand. Carrying this, she waded into the pond and began to paddle slowly toward the middle.

At the same time, Keith started climbing the birch tree nearest the water. Its trunk was strong at the base and became more and more slender as it reached the top. Keith climbed among the leaves, from branch to branch, until he was as close to the top as he could safely be and could feel the tree starting to bend under his weight. "I'm up!" he called to the girls below, and one by one they climbed the tree, too. With each climber, the tree bent farther, until Keith, at the top, was only a few yards from the surface of the water.

Then Amity made her dive. They all watched as her feet disappeared, and waited, holding their breath, until she came up. "Catch!" she cried, and she threw the rope to Keith, who tied it tightly to the tree trunk near the top.

Amity swam fast and waded ashore. "One at a time!" she called.

Neva, who'd been the last climber up, scooched back down. Oates came after her, then Celia. Each time a person stepped off, the tree trunk straightened up a little, pulling on the rope.

The rope was stretched tight, but nothing was coming up yet. "It might be too heavy," Amity said, disappointed. "Maybe we won't be able to get it."

Mandolyn came down next, and just as her feet touched the ground, the rope gave a jolt, and a loud crack sounded from under the water. A few bubbles blurped up. Quickly, Lottie jumped down, and Lulu came right after. Keith edged backward, gripping the tree, which was now fast unbending, its trunk groaning and squeaking as it tried to stand straight. When Keith's feet touched a low branch, he leapt to the ground.

The tree snapped upright. The rope rose and swung toward the shore. At the end of it, something draped in green slime rose with a splooch from the water.

"We got it!" Amity yelled.

"But what is it?" cried Lulu.

With a long branch, they pulled the rope toward the shore and undid the hook. The thing, whatever it was, thumped to the ground. They gathered around to look at it. Mandolyn wiped away the green slime.

"A circle," said Lulu. "Maybe a neck bone from a monster?"

Keith could see that it wasn't an animal. It was something human-made. He helped Mandolyn clean away the waterweeds, and they saw a circle the color of mud, with another, smaller circle inside it connected to the big circle by three parts, like a Y. Along the edges of the bigger circle were dents, and when Keith took hold of the thing, his fingers fit right into them.

"It's a steering wheel," he said. "Part of an ancient car that must be down there. You used it to make the car go right or left." He held the wheel with both hands and turned it back and forth in the air.

They all wanted to look closer, and to touch it, and to wonder.

"What's it doing in the pond?" Lulu asked.

Everyone looked at Keith for the answer. He shrugged. "Someone was going too fast," he said, "and took a wrong turn."

They thought the steering wheel should belong to Amity, since she discovered it. She took it home with her, cleaned it as best she could, and wrapped it in ribbons of many colors. She tied four strings to the wheel so she could hang it like a floating dinner plate from a beam over the roof garden of her house. The littlest birds, goldfinches and chickadees, seemed to like it. Sometimes three or four of them at once would perch there and make the ribbons flutter and the steering wheel swing.

A Note from the Author

More than thirty years ago, before many people were talking about solar power, I built a tiny solar-powered house. All its electricity came from two big panels standing in a field next to it. My computer, my lights, my fan, my hair dryer—all powered by the sun! I found this thrilling. Maybe soon, I thought, the sun would provide energy for the whole world.

It has turned out to be more complicated. Solar power has some fierce competition. For the last 150 years or so, human societies have been using the most powerful fuels we've ever discovered—coal, oil, and gas: the fossil fuels. We burn them to make electricity, we run our cars on them, we rely on them in our factories. Without them, we wouldn't have skyscrapers, cars, jet planes, rocket ships, computers, or the internet. We wouldn't have the modern world.

There's a problem with fossil fuels, though. Burning them sends a gas called carbon dioxide (CO_2) into the atmosphere. The more of that gas there is, the warmer the world gets, and the climate begins to act in strange ways. Terrifying wildfires blaze more often; heavy rainstorms cause floods. Heat waves push temperatures up and up, so high in some places that people can't work or even go outside. Polar ice melts, and the seas rise.

But because we want what our modern world offers, we keep using fossil fuels. We keep using them despite the rising heat and the fires and storms and floods. We keep using them, even though the long-term result could be an Earth that's uninhabitable for many forms of life, including the human race.

Our plan is to switch (eventually) to "renewable" energy—that is, energy that does no harm and that we'll never run out of, like energy from the sun, the wind, and the power of river currents. But these sources have their problems, too. As we know, the sun doesn't shine at night or on cloudy days; the wind isn't always blowing. We have batteries that can store electricity so we can use it when we need it. But we don't yet have batteries that can reliably store hours' or days' worth of electricity for large buildings or for cities or whole countries. That means renewables will not be our sole source of energy any time soon. Our plan, if it works at all, will work slowly. Meanwhile, the global temperature rises in a steep curve.

So we face hard questions: Will we stop using fossil fuels? Will we use them less? Will we figure out before it's too late how to power the world completely on renewable energy? If we do, what might that world look like?

For a long time—ever since I built that little one-room solar house—I have thought about these questions. I don't know the answers. I wrote *Project F* to imagine one way that things might turn out. Is it the best way? No. The best way wouldn't include a global catastrophe. But writing the book helped me think about what sort of world we might want, if we could start from scratch. What is most important? What could we do without? I think it's good to ask yourself big questions like these. Sooner or later, they could lead to some big answers.

About the Author

JEANNE DuPRAU is the *New York Times* bestselling author of the Books of Ember series. Her books have garnered numerous awards and have appeared on thirty state lists. *The City of Ember* was made into a feature movie in 2008. Jeanne lives in Northern California.